CW01507184

Acknowledgements

To all those people who helped me by getting this book published and by supplying information about those foreign places, weapons and training. They know who they are.

THE WRONG MAN

A work of fiction

THE
WRONG
MAN

Hamish Clarke

authorHOUSE®

AuthorHouse™ UK
1663 Liberty Drive
Bloomington, IN 47403 USA
www.authorhouse.co.uk
Phone: 0800.197.4150

Published by AuthorHouse 12/16/2014

ISBN: 978-1-4969-9893-4 (sc)
ISBN: 978-1-4969-9894-1 (e)

CHAPTER 1

A Bad Hut & an Even Worse Interview

My head hurt! I mean it really, really hurt; and, I could hear French; but it was French that I couldn't even start to understand. There was a dreadful smell!

Yes, French voices but with very definite African accents. I had done French at school, but la plume de ma tante is not much bloody use in Africa!

I was desperately thirsty and I desperately needed a leak. And I hurt whenever I moved. I knew that I was in Hell, and I hadn't even opened my eyes.

I got my act together enough to open my eyes and look around. I was in a very small room with metal walls and roof. Bars on the window. Dirt floor. It was obviously a prefabricated metal hut. It was round with a single metal door. The smell was coming from the single item in the hut, a rusty bucket. This was to be my toilet - great! Well, at least I could have my much needed slash.

I looked through the bars and all I could see was the back of a similar hut and dust and part of a tree. Grey brown branches with a mass of sun bleached and water washed pale grey/green leaves. I pinched myself to see if I was dreaming.

Ouch! No I wasn't. Yes, this was Africa, the tree, the dust, the glaring sun and the accents all agreed.

I could hear a new language, but we didn't do African languages at school. Fat lot of use an expensive English education when you are in the shit in Africa. Still, what to do? Don't do anything stupid, there are obviously no British Bobbies around here to ask the time."

"This was Uganda; but they speak English in Uganda. But they are speaking French. What the hell was going on?"

I calmed down. What assets did I have? Well, I had my Out of Africa clothing; you know, the safari jacket in earth colours but I had lost my lightweight boots. I had heard that shoes were in such short supply in Africa that the first things to go were your footwear. The only thing left in my pockets was my handkerchief.

No passport, money, traveller's cheques, watch, Swiss army knife (penknives were still allowed in the UK and on planes, in those days), notebook or pencil. Had I been robbed before I got here, wherever that was? I had my clothes and that was it!

This was the archetypal horror scene in the adventure movies, and I was living it!

I felt that I was dying of thirst, so I knew that I had better do something about it. I banged on the door. Nothing. After a minute, I banged on the door again. Still nothing. I knew that people were around because I could still hear the Africanized French and the local language.

It took great patience but I counted to six hundred before I tried again. Success! I knew that in a third world country, the one thing that you don't do, is piss off your captors.

The door opened and a very large African in a faded blue uniform opened started shouting at me in very rapid French. Unfortunately he was really pissed off! Oops. In my best schoolboy French I apologised and asked for water. I left it at that, I thought, One thing at a time."

He left muttering about Americans, slamming the door. I don't think he was still angry, it merely required the door to be slammed if it was to be closed.

It seemed like an eternity, but was probably only about five minutes later when the door was wrenched open again, but by an old man in rags carrying an earthenware jug and cup. He put them down, saying nothing and then left, slamming the door again. Thank God, water. I got the jug into the light and looked in. Yuk, the water was a pale milky colour - clay? Well, at least the clay may adsorb some of the nasties and I did have a handkerchief. I filtered the water. It tasted musty but at least I was no longer dying of thirst. But maybe I would die of dysentery, but that would be later.

I waited. And waited, and waited.

I slept.

I am not sure if it was the squadrons of mosquitoes dive bombing me or the arrival of some sort of diesel powered truck which woke me, but was night. I took some more water, filtering it as best as I could as there was only moonlight to see by. I left some. I didn't know when I would be given my next ration. And now, I was hungry. How long had I been here? My stomach told me that I hadn't eaten in days.

Maybe I should have left the clay and other bits in the water, it would have given me something to chew on. The stink in the hut was also worse, I had been using my five star plumbing - the bucket.

The door screeched open. A different faded blue uniform beckoned me to follow him. I followed.

I looked around as I followed him. There was sufficient moonlight to see two rows of small round huts, set in a semi-circle. There were a couple of pick-ups at the centre. Trees surrounded this grouping. In the middle distance, in the direction that the semi - circle was facing, were a spattering of tiny lights. I could see candles flickering in some of the huts and the vastly stronger light of some sort of lamp coming from one of the huts. This is where I was being led.

Great! I was in or near to a town with no electricity. A power cut or a town in the middle of nowhere?

I entered the one dome of brightness for what appeared to be hundreds of miles. There was a large metal desk, and sitting behind was a man in an immaculately laundered white shirt covered by a bad taste tie which almost shouted at you. Standing behind him was the first uniformed African who I had seen.

I had a better chance to see the uniform. It was originally dark blue. Combat jacket, trousers and boots. But what was interesting was that he didn't have a belt but a rope wrapped around him held together with a shackle. This rope held a holster.

I now knew which country that I was in. I had seen uniforms like this before on the news. This was a Zairean Gendarme's uniform. I was being held by the Zairean police. And I still didn't know why or how I got there?

All this happened before Kabila got on the scene. This was still the Mobutu era. I was in the deep smelly stuff and I couldn't swim.

Despite the benches next to the walls, I was made to sit on the floor. The man in the white shirt started to speak to me in very rapid French and started to get angry when I didn't respond. The schoolboy French came to my rescue again. He quietened down when he realised that I had not understood him. He started to speak to me in English with a Texan accent. Now I understood the mutterings about Americans. He told me that he had been trained in Texas, but he didn't tell me what he had been trained in. I was soon to find out and I would not like it one bit!

Still sitting, he started to slap a pair of pliers into the palm of his left hand. Smiling, "You will tell the truth." Oh yes, I really was in the crap!

Wham! someone had hit me across the back of the head without warning. I didn't even know that he was there. White shirt smiled again and said, "This is a taste of what's to come if you don't speak the truth. In my opinion, traditional African methods of obtaining the truth are better than American methods which are far too slow." I was about to dye my underpants brown and would have told him anything. I was terrified.

He started, "What are you doing in Zaire? Where were the diamonds, drugs and weapons? He went on, Where are your accomplices?" He was still smiling and slapping that pair of pliers into his left hand. I said goodbye to my balls whilst I was still conscious. I couldn't answer him, how could I? I didn't know what the hell he was talking about.

Wham! another blow to the head. I told him what I knew which sounded pretty fake to me, and it had happened to me. I didn't even know what day of the week it was. Again, 'What are you doing in Zaire? Where were the diamonds, drugs and weapons?" and again, "Where are your accomplices?"

"Look I'm not stupid. If I knew what was going on, I'd tell you. The last thing I remember is sitting by the side of the road in Uganda, on my way to see the gorillas. Then I woke up here". He just continued smiling and slapping those pliers into his palm.

And wham! another blow to the head. "Where is your passport, your money, dollars? You're a spy and all spies carry at least two passports and lots of dollars, so where are they? Why were you just lying by the side of the road when you were found by the Gendarmes?" O.K., I had been robbed before the cops found me. Wonderful, I get another piece of information but I was soon going to become an unmale.

I was getting really scared. I told him my story again and he got up without a word. I expected them to strip me but no, he just started to crush the joints of my right fingers one by one with those bloody pliers.

I am not a superhero. The pain inflicted by a pair of pliers on finger joints is unbearable. Don't let anybody kid you, if you have anything to say, you'll say it. I blacked out I don't know how many times, only to be woken up by blows to the head and kicks to the chest and stomach. If I had had anything to say, I would have said it!

After he had worked on three fingers, he realised that I was telling the truth or that I was James Bond.

Suddenly, they stopped. I was given water, then whiskey, then food. Everybody was very jolly, but no apologies. They started to take down details of my story, but they never told me exactly where I was or Mr. White Shirt's name. I was then led back to my cell, and miracle of miracles, there were my boots.

I was woken up next morning, given food, water and a chance to wash. I was taken to the pick-up that I had heard the previous night and made to sit in it. The big Gendarme and Mr. White Shirt got in on either side of me. I didn't realise how big and tough Mr. White Shirt was, until he sat next to me. His muscles had muscles. The big Gendarme was driving.

We drove away from the town that I had glimpsed that night. What the hell was going on now? My hand still hurt like crazy, so I am ashamed to admit that I didn't take much notice of the journey. I felt every bump on the road and the journey seemed to go on for ever.

I do remember that whenever anybody saw that pick-up, they got off the road. Mr. White Shirt was obviously bad, bad news, but I had found that out from personal experience. I did not like his Southern hospitality one bit.

They were both very nice and polite and I still didn't know what was going on. All I was expecting was a 9mm or a 7.62mm hole in the back of the head. That was if I was lucky; I noticed two pangas in the back of the pick-up when I got in. What was worrying was that the rust appeared blood coloured. I was not a happy chappy.

I became a really unhappy chappy when we stopped about ten kilometres out of town. I really thought that this was the end and I looked for a place to run, if I got the chance. Thankfully, it wasn't necessary. I was informed with much laughter that this was where I had been found. They obviously realised what I had been thinking - big joke.

We stopped again about five hundred meters further on. Again, we did not get out. "What do you know about this?"

I looked around, "About what?" I looked again and in the bushes by the side of the road I could see a Land Cruiser but no rust, so it had only just happened. I looked again, yes, those were bullet holes, a bloody great swarm of the things, all down one side. I could also see why they were pissed off; the logo had something about, Du President on it. Somebody had shot up a presidential vehicle, and I was their only suspect, oh shit!

Had I been in the ambush? That would explain the bruises.

Luckily, they realised just like before, that all this was new to me. I was patted on the shoulder and asked about my fingers. Mr. White Shirt smiled, "I'm very good at what I do so don't worry, you'll fully recover." Great!

We stopped twice before our destination. Both times for beers, or at least they had beers, I had Coke. There was no way that I wanted to get drunk; I might say something really stupid. Eventually, I started to realise that someone who was much more important than Mr. White Shirt, wanted to see me. I slowly started to relax.

The whole journey took about four hours. That didn't help - I still didn't know where I was, how far from Uganda? But I did manage to work out was that it was three days after the punctured tyre in Uganda. I had lost one and a half days. What they hell had happened?

We suddenly arrived. With very little warning, we drove through a couple of villages, and of course, as before, everybody scampered out of the way. Mr. White Shirt was obviously well known and well loved; ha! ha! It was a large airport. And there on the Tarmac was a Boeing 737 in Zairean Airways colours.

We drove straight to it, and I was made to get out of the pick-up and get in at the rear of the plane. The last six rows were empty and I was made to sit in the last row. None of the other passengers looked at me; I didn't exist. Mr. White Shirt passed me on to two clones of himself. He told me not to expect any stewardess service or to talk to his clones as everybody was under orders not to talk to me. We took off without delay. It seems that the plane was waiting just for me; lucky me.

Why was it that everyone who I had met since being in Zaire was built like a brick shithouse? The only guy smaller than me was the old man in rags who had brought me water.

Still, I was given some water and food on the plane. I think that they thought that it would keep me quiet. It did. The plane trip gave me a chance to reflect on what was happening to me.

CHAPTER 2

Amanda & Gorillas

"The clouds rolled down the valley like cigar smoke wafting over the green baize of a billiard table," or some such bullshit. Forget it; it wasn't like that at all!

Actually, it all started with Amanda. We first met at the office Christmas party. She made straight for me. and within a week, she had moved in. I thought that I was the luckiest man in the world.

I should have known better - I've always had bad luck with blondes.

I had had to work bloody hard to reach the position that I had; I am a scientist, and after fifteen years of hard work working for an engineering consultancy, I was a team leader; doing an interesting and responsible job and starting to get reasonable money. If the project went well, I had a real chance of breaking through the glass ceiling; of being offered a Partnership in the firm.

Then Amanda comes into my life. She's a civil engineer and bright too.

To cut a long story short, she was passing all my ideas on to Harry, one of the partners, and she was sleeping with anybody who could advance her career. It is amazing how stupid a man can be when he doesn't think with his brains.

One day, I was called into Harry's office. Yes, you've guessed it, I was to be removed from the team and guess who was to be the new team leader? Right again; it was to be Amanda. I was incompetent, Amanda had all the brains and had come up with all the ideas, etc., etc..

Big, big row at home that night. Thankfully, she let the cat out of the bag about sleeping with Harry. I got the evidence which I needed, so next day, I stormed into the partner's office and another big row ensued. I got what I wanted: a good retrenchment package and an excellent reference. Sometimes, I do what is in my best interests.

I cleared out my desk, collected my retrenchment cheque and had a long word with the senior partner. It appeared that he knew what had been going on, but could do nothing because he had effectively retired; he suggested that I attend a conference in Kenya on the firm's behalf, at company expense, and go on holiday immediately afterwards. Robert really is a good sort.

Due to Robert's efforts, I was offered two jobs; the first in York, working for a small consultancy and the second in the Manchester office of a large international consultancy, with a chance of several overseas projects. Either way, I would have to sell the flat in Surbiton, but there was always a demand for property in London.

Needless to say, the conference was a disappointment. It was full of bureaucrats; lots of good food and drink, with considerable amounts of hot air and no decisions.

I decided to change my plans and go and visit the Gorillas in the Mist I hopped on a flight to Entebbe. Despite some confusion over which was my hire car, I was on my way to Bwindi Impenetrable Park to see the Gorillas. I never got there.

We had just passed through Mbarara when we got a puncture. Replacing the tyre was what I would find to be a typical African experience, the spare was flat. The last thing I remember was seeing the driver rolling the spare tyre back down the road to a garage about five kilometres back. I got back into the car and waited...

Then my police cell. Nothing in between.

At least that was behind me. On the plus side, I was on a 'plane for Kinshasa where there would be a British Consulate who would help me. I had found that out from the hostey's announcement. I was bruised but not permanently damaged. I could just move the fingers of my right hand. I knew which country I was in and what day of the week it was. The Plane had been held up for me so somebody wanted me alive for the meantime.

CHAPTER 3

Luxury & Squalor

On the minus side, I was under arrest in a country with a dubious legal system - I wasn't even within the criminal justice system! I had no money or documents. I couldn't account for being in the country. I was somehow involved in the ambush of a presidential vehicle. When I added up all the pluses and minuses, I reckoned that I was in the pooh.

Still, I was on my way to Kinshasa and there was a British Consulate in Kinshasa. If I could get word to them, they would sort out this mess and I could go home. I would take the low key job in York, I had had enough of foreign parts. So maybe things weren't so bad after all.

It was still daylight when we landed in what was obviously Kinshasa. The River Congo is bloody wide. You can see it as you come in to land. Not a fun landing, as there were potholes on the runway.

As soon as the plane landed, a car drew up along side and I was invited to get in. There were people outside the terminal building waiting to identify their luggage before getting onto an international flight, but there was no chance of speaking to them unless I wanted to be dead. At least, that is the impression that I got.

We drove straight out of the airport into town. An interesting drive. It took thirty minutes despite the sirens. The roads varied from fair to appalling. My two goons were replaced by two more Mr. White Shirt clones. However, these two felt free to speak. They appeared decent and we spoke a mixture of French and English, but I wasn't taken in. I knew that they could be as ruthless as anybody else that I had met.

We passed a half built re-enforced concrete copy of the Eiffel Tower, only bigger. It appears that the money had been eaten i.e. corruption during the project. We also passed three madmen lying in the middle of the road. A great deal of jocularity but great care not to harm them - that would be bad luck. As I said, an interesting journey.

I was absolutely astonished when we arrived at a hotel, and to find that it was the Inter-Continental. I had been booked in that morning and I could go straight up to my room without needing to sign in. My initial thought was to have a bath, then I used my brains; but in hindsight, I didn't. I found no goons in the room and I realised that I could make local calls direct. I immediately called the British Consulate and told them the story. "Don't worry," the operator said, "We'll be right along."

I had a long bath which helped the bruising and went downstairs. Yes my bill would be paid in full and I could have anything that I wanted. Great, I got a couple of hours sleep, while waiting for the Foreign Office boys or girls, then went down to dinner.

I had a drink in the bar first, and noticed some Embassy types. I told them my woes. Their attitude was, "Look, old chap, this is not really our problem. It's a Consulate matter and we're Trade, but we'll pass it on."

"For god? sake help me." I begged, "I don't know what happened to me, I've been tortured for information I don't know anything about, and these bastards can pick me up again at any time!"

They were getting irritated. "I've told you, it's not our problem. Anyway why did you have to come out to Africa; you know it's dangerous. If you wanted to go on holiday, why didn't you go to Spain like everybody else, the Costa del Sol? It's safe there. You people always cause problems when you come out to places like this. This isn't Surbiton, you know." I realised that if I stayed talking to them, I would be doing myself more harm than good.

Then it dawned on me. They were archetypal school prefects. The ex-public school types were just like the ones who tried to get me to bend over, in private, at school. I thought that the ex-state school types may save me but they were trying to be just like the ex-public school types. No hope of help at all.

After Philby and Blunt, I thought that the Foreign Office may have learnt its lesson but apparently not. After dinner, I went up to my room and tried the Consulate again. "Terribly sorry, but the duty officer was at a very important cocktail party. We'll be with you first thing tomorrow morning." I went to bed, my bruises needed the rest.

Before breakfast, I had found a map. My best guess was that I had been found to the east of Kisangani, which put the ambush about four hundred kilometres to the west of the Ugandan border. Luckily, I had a chance to finished breakfast downstairs before my two goons arrived. I was again invited to go with them. You didn't mess with these boys, even in an international hotel.

We got into the same luxury car and went to a very large and austere building in the centre of town. I soon found out that this was a Police headquarters. Everybody was very polite until I was locked in a cell. My round metal hut was luxury compared to this place. The floor was concrete and a running sewer. There was nothing in the room, not even a window, just a fluorescent light which was switched on and off apparently at random. I waited.

I couldn't stand forever. I had to sit down; it was too wet to lie down and I'd probably get pneumonia. At last I had dyed my underpants brown, but it wasn't of my making. The floor really was an ankle deep sewer.

Then they came for me. It must have been about four hours later, by the state of my thirst. I was led to a huge room with a single stool in the centre. There were four of them, Mr. White Shirt clones, except one was somewhat older. He said nothing but just watched expressionlessly. The others all spoke with a Texan accent; surprise, surprise.

It was the same questions, all over again. I think that they must have taken me to the hotel to psychologically soften me up. I don't know why but it didn't. Firstly, I hadn't done anything wrong and secondly, I had somehow expected this.

This time they didn't use pliers. It was high tech, a mixture of injections which both caused agony and drowsiness and electric shock. You know that I said that I wasn't Rambo, well, I'm more like wimpo. The interrogation went on for what seemed like weeks but was probably only hours, or at most a couple of days. I spent most of the time screaming or blacked out. Then it stopped.

I woke up naked in my cell. I waited, and waited. Nothing. Everything that should have been there was there, and nothing was broken and my hand was getting better, just more bruises. Mr. White Shirt was right, they were good!

They came again. Only this time, I was pushed under a shower and given a bar of soap. I was then taken to another cell. This time it was clean with another rusty bucket, but it had a bed with a single blanket and a window, with bars of course. I stayed there for five days. They even fed me twice a day. Revolting food but it was food.

On the sixth day, they took me back to the showers, where I was allowed to shave under supervision and then they gave me back my clothes which had been cleaned and pressed. I even got my boots back, also cleaned. What was going on? I soon found out.

I had just finished dressing when the door opened. It was Her Majesty's representative. "Terribly sorry," he apologised, "But I've been awfully busy. Anyway, it's your fault for getting involved in this business."

"What bloody business?" I was already pissed off by his attitude and I wanted to know what was going on. He was supposed to be helping me.

"If you don't know already, its better that you stay not knowing.". he said. "There's a trade deal coming up, and you're rocking the boat." What a bastard! "Look, I've seen you, and you seem O.K.. These stories of torture that you're telling are nonsense. I know that these people are a bit rough, but they're not going to harm a British tourist unless he's up to no good." What no good? Is being tortured for no reason, up to no good? "You're not injured, just a little bruised but they're obviously looking after you well. The cell is clean, you're being fed and you've got clean clothes, so you're obviously exaggerating."

He looked around again. "I've done my bit. I've checked that your O.K. and not being abused. I'll be on my way. Keep your nose clean and you'll be fine. Chin up! and then he left. He was an archetypal wannabe prefect type.

I was shocked. The representatives of H.M.G. were not going to lift a finger to help me. I was on my own. If anybody was going to get me out of this mess, it was going to be me. I still didn't know what it was all about and it was obvious that the goons were still convinced that I was a key player. How obviously, showed itself immediately.

The more elderly goon came in, the one who said nothing during my interrogation. He started to speak in English. Yes you've guessed it, he also had the perfect Texan accent. I was under control of Texan speaking Congolese. What gives?

"Y'all knows what? going on. I'd be real obliged if y'all tell me. I know that y'all know about the briefcase." It had to be of great value, or they would have just chucked me out of the country after the visit by that idiot from the Consulate Office. But why was I kidnapped and taken four hundred kilometres into Zaire? This chain of thought was stopped by Y'all.

"Look ah don't have no choice. If y'all don't tell what ah need to know, ah won't have no need to keep y'all alive. I still didn't know what they wanted to know, otherwise I would have told them or made something up. Ah'm going to give y'all one last chance." He looked deeply into my eyes. "The two of us is going back to Kisangani, and then we'll see that ambush one last time. It'll help y'all remember, and if y'all don't talk; well?" Now, I really was scared. "We're going now."

I needed to think, but I didn't have time.

The same old luxury car with the same old flashing lights and siren, with the same two goons were there to take us to the airport. We met the same three madmen lying across the road, but this time there were no comments about the half built monument and the eating of the funds.

For the return trip, I was honoured by the use of an executive jet. Maybe Y'all didn't like public transport. The two goons came with us to keep me in line. It was interesting to note that they were terrified of Y'all. In fact all the Congolese who we came into contact with, cowered before Y'all. A very powerful man.

We had a shorter and therefore better take off than the previous landing. At last, I could think. I knew that they were going to kill me, and no-one cared. I was expected to die for a bunch of old broken down London buses. Bugger them, I decided that I wasn't going to die if I could help it.

Up till now, I had had a fairly mundane and conformist life for someone of my background. I was the product of reasonably wealthy parents. I was not a great student but I was fortunate in that I was able to get a degree in earth and environmental sciences. While I was studying, I thought I would be a real hero and joined the T.A., the British Army Reserves. By the end of my studies, I had managed to con a commission out Her Majesty, and I had joined a T.A. Sapper unit.

I had done the usual things including the two week special to arms Royal Engineers officers' instant experts' course and became a troop commander. I really thought that we were the bees knees. I did a couple of other courses but after three or four years, the pressure of work, which was considerable, encouraged me to leave. Luckily before I left, I had managed to get a few weeks in the jungle in Belize and a chance to attend a few lectures and exercises on escape, evasion and what to do if captured. I found out that I was no hero - so much for dreams of being Rambo. Anyway, the Belize trip taught me that I was a joke compared my regular counterparts, and I think this is what really decided me to leave.

The E & E lectures taught us one thing - don't piss off your captors! But I didn't need to be told this, I had been to an expensive public school. It was run just like a prison, with the guards being the school prefects. A crueller bunch of bastards you couldn't find anywhere on the planet. This is why British ex-public school types do so well in prison - just like school. And if you have homosexual tendencies, life becomes easy. I didn't have those tendencies, so life was unbelievably hard, especially since I was not athletic.

The E & E lectures taught us other things. They said be polite but firm, well, I had been polite and a wimp. I noticed that all the goons had started to take me for granted, even Mr. White Shirt on our trip to the airport. Stay a wimp until the opportunity arises. The lectures stated that an opportunity arises as long as you look for it. They also stated that you must get you hands on anything that may possibly help your escape or subsequent evasion, however stupid it may seem. They also taught us that opportunities to escape don't come often, so if you see an opportunity, take it; it may be the only one you'll get.

We even had stewardess service on the flight. Great, I drank water like no tomorrow. Thankfully, no-one thought this unusual. I ate twice, I suppose that they thought that it was a case of the condemned man eating a hearty breakfast. In reality, if I escaped I would need as much energy as I could get if I was going to outrun their bullets.

I managed to secrete one set of plastic cutlery up a sleeve and two packets of sweet biscuits in a pocket. All I would need would be water. O.K. I had done all I could at this stage; the worm was beginning to turn. I had to turn, I had no other choice except graciously accept my own murder - fat chance and stuff the trade deal!

No-one was going to make money out of my death! The worm really was turning. Unfortunately, there was nothing I could do on the plane. Even if I could disable all the goons and the stewardess, and she was a huge hunk of muscle - lots to hang onto, I'd still have the flight crew to deal with. I couldn't fly and I doubted that there was enough fuel to get to Uganda, and I seriously doubted that there were parachutes on board. I would have to wait until we landed.

So what did I know? Some person or persons unknown had shanghaied me four hundred kilometres into Zaire and left me for dead 500m from an ambushed presidential vehicle. A secret police organisation was running around like a headless chicken looking for something which was of great value.

Even when I was in the T.A., I realised that few countries have any real secrets from any other country. Government secrets are to be kept from their own populations. So, these thugs were not looking for a great secret, anyway, they were internal security. It must be an object or objects.

It couldn't be wealth in the form of money or diamonds, Y'all was actively involved in the search. Zaire was awash with diamonds and Y'all must have had easier ways of getting diamonds or dollars. And if it were, he wouldn't trust anybody else with disposable wealth and Mr. White Shirt was alone initially. No, it had to be something else. But what?

My mind kept on coming back to the ambush. A presidential vehicle had been used for something, and it had been shot up. That Toyota was brand new, so they were ensuring that there would be no mechanical breakdowns. It was carrying something and/or somebody important. O.K., whatever it was could not have been heavy or large, otherwise the goons would have used a truck. It must be very special, otherwise they would have used a normal army escort. What would be so secret? It couldn't be plans, because it would have already been made or they didn't have the capability to make it and anyway they could have been faxed or e-mailed. O.K., so we come back to a small lightweight object.

Drugs? Why bring them into the country via Uganda, There were better ways. And if drugs, why was I involved? No, not drugs. The only thing that I could think of, was a weapon of mass destruction. It couldn't be nuclear. Once off devices, so too many suitcases. But chemical or biological would suit and it wouldn't be easily noticed by the outside world, if used. Biological is uncontrollable. The bugs evolve into more devastating forms, or useless forms or back into the original species.

No, it had to be chemical, or Red Mercury (I'd seen a documentary on it). My guess was chemical, to be used against any rebel forces. After all, what is an African army for but to suppress its own population.

They would still need an expert and someone must have mistaken me for the relevant expert. Come to think of it, the last thing I remembered in Uganda was a sort of hissing. That's it, I had been kidnapped in the belief that I was the expert. The puncture was a set up job and I was gassed. So that's how it was done. That would also explain why I was out for over thirty six hours.

I was probably lying on the floor of the Land Cruiser when it got hit, but all the bullets went too high; untrained troops or anybody else for that matter, tend to shoot high at night. And being unconscious, I was relaxed enough to survive the crash. But how did I get five hundred meters up the road. Another survivor or an ambusher?.

But why was I left? If by a survivor, was he or she wounded or injured and too weak to continue carrying me? Or was I set up to replace the genuine expert? If so, did the ambushers move me just to muddy the waters, or did someone take pity on me and hope that I would recover in time and get away?

Were the Brits involved? No, although indifferent to the welfare of other Brits, this deception would require more subtlety than the prefects have. One only has to look at the M.I.6 Latvian operation. That was a cock-up from start to finish. Anyway, if they did think this one up, they would have got me out of the country when I was in Kinshasa, in case I gave the game away by the fact that I did not know anything.

Could all these Texan goons be in the pay of the C.I.A.? Possibly, they must have spent a long time in the states, and even the F.B.I. would have caught on. But their training may have been part of the U.S.'s efforts to contain the communist menace in Africa. I kept an open mind on that hypothesis. Still, I still didn't like their interpretation of hospitality. And they did plan to kill me, perhaps only to cover their tracks?

And where there are weapons, there are Russians. There is a regular direct Interflot flight to Moscow from Entebbe. I saw the aeroplane when I landed there myself. Russian Mafia selling chemical weapons or that great mystery, Red Mercury. Were they supposed to meet the expert in Uganda prior to crossing to Zaire? Were the K.G.B., or whatever they are called now, to try and stop this operation. After all the Russians in the form of the G.R.U. are the greatest deception planners of all time, better even than than the Chinese. Hmm, I'd keep an open mind on that one as well.

What about a joint operation, to stop a madman from getting hold of a weapon of mass destruction. No, that only happens in the movies.

So far, so good. But first I had to escape and find that wounded survivor, if there was one. But first I had to escape!

We had to fasten our seat belts as we would be landing shortly. The wimp, me, asked if I could have some of the bottled water for the road trip to the ambush site, as I didn't drink beer. They thought this really unmanly and so were really happy to say yes. I took three litres, any more would have been suspicious. O.K., now I had the water, all I needed was a plan and an opportunity. Well, I had started.

We landed, but this time, we were travelling in a Nissan Patrol. It must have been for Y'all's benefit.

Anyway, it was a much more pleasant journey back to the Ambush site. We didn't stop for beers, so I had to drink some of the water to keep in character. I had two litres left when we arrived at the Ambush site. And I still hadn't escaped. Oh, shit, I was going to die if I didn't do something quickly and there was nothing I could do in the car, being surrounded by goons.

I had to think up a plan to escape, and guess what, I couldn't think of a thing that would work, and now I my bladder was really bursting after all that water and, oh yeah, don't forget the fear.

CHAPTER 4

Thanks for the Memory & Breakfast with Tiffany

Well, here we were again. I needed to get out of the Nissan, both to have that leak, I was getting so desperate that I couldn't think and because I had no chance of escape whilst I remained in the car.

They started to ask me the same old questions, but thankfully without violence. We just sat there with the aircon running full blast. They really didn't want to get out into the heat. This may be my chance. I showed them my empty water bottles, and with my real show of fear, they realised that I was almost wetting myself with fear. They really didn't need me pissing myself in the car; that would mean opening the windows to get rid of the smell and to let the seats dry. No way, that would mean no aircon!

One of the goons got out of the car with me. I held on as long as I could; I needed to look around and I needed them to think that despite being near to bursting, I was so nervous that I couldn't pee. The goon was sweating like a pig, me too but that didn't matter. Bingo, the forest on the other side of the track to the ambushed Land Cruiser was thick enough to make shooting difficult. These goons were good at whatever they did, so they could probably shoot like Annie Oakley. I needed to get into cover before they could draw and fire.

We were standing in the shade by the Patrol with everybody watching me. I shrugged, and they realised I couldn't perform what Nature intended. I zipped up, crossed the road and unzipped again. This time I stood in the sun. Then relief! Oh, boy, there really is nothing like it! They were cracking up with laughter; they were almost wetting themselves and the goon outside could barely stand up, he was laughing so much.

Good! I ran! I didn't even zip up, I just ran. I ran straight into the trees. It must have taken a good five seconds before the first shout went up, and another two to three seconds before the first shot went off, but by that time, I was into cover. I zipped up, because if I didn't I was going to get scratched in a very painful place! I kept on running.

I was not fit, they were, but they weren't running for their lives - I was. Oh, Shit! I nearly ran straight into a Gabon Viper. These are huge snakes with fangs two inches long, difficult to see in amongst the forest litter. But thank God, they hiss when threatened and are not that aggressive if you go round them. Thanks brother, you have given me an idea. All the goons and the driver were getting out of the car, but my pee watcher was catching up. Ha! ha! He almost stepped on brother snake as well. He stopped and then started running more cautiously, by the sound of it. He no longer sounded like an express train. He had also stopped shooting after the initial five rounds. Thank God for that.

I felt like I was dying, there was no way that I could keep running. If I started to walk, the goons would soon catch me up and find me; I had to hide, but hide successfully. Then suddenly, in front was a dense bush sitting right next to a large tree. It was just the place that a snake would hide away from the sun. Well, I had to chance it. I rolled under the bush, causing the least disturbance possible to the forest litter. Joy, oh joy, no snakes. I could only pray that the goons were townies and not alert country boys. I really hoped that this secret police unit did not offer tracking courses. No need to worry, my pee watcher ran straight past my hiding place.

The second goon ran past, carrying a pistol. Then Y'all came up. He was carrying an A.K.; He had taken the time to get the right equipment to take me out, no fool Y'all. Oh, Shit; he stopped two meters from where I was almost dyeing my underpants brown again. He then started to poke the bush with the barrel of the A.K.. I said he was no fool; I don't suppose you get to be a powerful bastard like him if you're an idiot.

What do brother Gabon Vipers do under these circumstances? They hiss. I became Hissing Sid with a vengeance. Y'all decided that discretion was the better part of valour, and that I wasn't under my bush. He left to follow the others who were shouting to each about something.

So far, so good. No! not so far, not so good! The driver was walking and following my tracks. He was a middle aged man who was obviously not a goon. He must have been a country boy. He was also only the second person who I had met in Zaire who was smaller than me.

I needed a weapon. The fates must have been on my side because on the other side of the bush from the driver, lay a branch that must had been made for the purpose. I slowly and quietly rolled out from under the bush and grabbed the branch. I waited, crouching behind the bush. He just stood there looking at the bush. Come on, if I stay crouching like this much longer, I won't be able to move. My lungs were still agony, and my desire to pant was excruciating. I waited.

At last, he walked up to the bush. It was obvious to me that he hadn't been trained, but he carried a nasty little snub nosed revolver which I thought was quite a good substitute for training, especially when all I had was a branch. He got on his hands and knees and stuck his head under the bush to look properly. I moved. I doubt that I have ever moved so fast before or since, in my life. I was round that bush so fast that all he could do was to turn his head to look at me; he didn't even shout. I hit him over the head as hard as I could with my bespoke branch. The worm really had turned.

Bugger! My branch had just turned to dust - it was rotten! He blinked and I just started to kick and punch as hard, as fast and as often as I could. He didn't utter a sound, but just kept on gripping that snubby which he kept on trying to point at me. He was concentrating so hard on shooting me that he didn't even try to defend himself. By luck more than good judgement, I kicked him first in the stomach, then on the chin. He was out. I then punched him but I think I hurt me more than I hurt him. He really was out for the count.

I searched him. He had that snubby, eight spare rounds and ten dollars in one dollar bills. Nothing else was any use. He didn't have the keys to the Nissan on him. I took the snubby, the spare ammo and the dollars and then rolled him into my hiding place. I was now armed and dangerous! I looked at the revolver; it was a five shot Smith & Wesson Chiefs Special with a two inch barrel. I was in luck, a serviceable firearm. Now what to do? I jogged back to the Nissan. If the keys were still in the vehicle, I was away and clear, on my way to Uganda. No chance, the bloody doors were locked; Y'all must have the keys. I said that he was no idiot.

"Right, think!" I was up against three bruisers who were bigger, fitter and more ruthless than me. They had at least two handguns and an A.K.. They were used to fighting in this environment; I had never fought in my life, only played at it. Well, this is for real, and I had better win this game! Now what? I could bugger off, stay by the Nissan and ambush 'The Wild Bunch' - fat chance, or take the goons on one by one. If I buggered off, they would catch me; they could always call in the Army to search for me. I had no chance trying to ambush them; they were too professional, and I could forget playing Rambo with them in the forest, besides it wasn't thick enough. It was tropical forest not thick jungle.

The first thing I had to do was to stop any form of communications with outside assets. I broke off the two aerials on the Nissan. It was just the four of us now. Now what? Stop losing it! Calm down. O.K., O.K.. I had to reduce the odds against me. I couldn't break into the Nissan and hot-wire it. Firstly, it would be too noisy and time consuming, they would get back before I could leave, and secondly, I didn't know how to hot-wire a car. They didn't teach us that at school, or in the T.A.. Must write and tell them to change the curriculum, essential knowledge for the middle class twit in Africa!

I was still dithering when I heard shouts about one hundred meters away but the goons must have been about fifty meters apart and then a burst of fire from the A.K. about three of four hundred meters away. They were running around at random looking for me. Maybe I had a chance. Then a different voice, the driver must have regained consciousness; I'd forgotten about him. Make that four people that I was up against. Oh shit, they knew that I was armed.

I carefully walked back in the direction of my old hiding place. One of the goons was talking to the driver. The driver then went trotting off in the general direction of the burst of fire. The idiot goon started to run straight towards me. At the last moment, one meter away, he saw me. It was too late, I gave him a .38 special third nostril. I threw up. This was the first life that I had ever taken. I had never even had to point a gun at anybody before.

Get a grip! I searched him. This guy did not look after his firearm. It was rusted to hell. I could barely take out the magazine or work the slide. It was going to jam! The ammunition in the magazine was O.K. though. What else. I took his watch, money about a hundred dollars, his spare magazine which was full and appeared in good condition and his lighter. No car keys. He did have a quarter pint bottle of brandy; I took that too. All the rest was junk. He didn't even have a penknife.

Movement, I moved back into the shadows. Ah, my friend the driver. He didn't see me but he saw the dead goon and where I had thrown up. He took one look and ran back the way that he had come. I couldn't believe it but the second goon did exactly what the first goon had done but from the other direction. He also got a .38 special nostril but from two meters. I was improving and I didn't throw up this time.

I had to be quick because the A.K. was coming at a great rate on knots, although I thought that Y'all would be more cautious. I quickly searched the second goon. This one was prepared. His pistol was a Browning High-Power, just like his colleague. The surface was worn but otherwise in immaculate condition. His spare magazine was also in excellent condition. He had a sort of fighting clasp knife and one of those tool knives with pliers. He also had about one hundred and fifty dollars in cash; strange, no-one carried local currency. There was a small pad of tissues and a porno magazine in his jacket pocket. I took the lot, even his cheap wrist watch, it may come in useful. He had a holster and spare magazine pouch on his belt, they were nice but the belt was poor quality, mine was better.

I stuffed everything into the pockets of my jacket, except the Browning which went into my waistband, and ran to the Nissan. And waited in the shadows.

I had achieved the impossible. I had knocked out the driver, who was now being very cautious, wise man. I had killed two goons and stripped them of most of their useful items. How to deal with Y'all? It was obvious to me that he was more dangerous than all the other goons that I met, put together. Concurrent activity; use the time to think or do something!

I stripped the well looked after Browning. Yes it was in good shape. I emptied all the magazines and reloaded the three good ones with the best quality ammunition. I had been a soldier, albeit a week-end warrior. You don't forget your basic drills! I reloaded the S&W and sorted out the rest of the kit. I holstered the Browning and I was ready to go. I looked into the back of the Nissan. I looked again, I couldn't believe my eyes. The barrel of an M 79 40mm grenade launcher was peeking out from under the carpet. I just had to have it! I could beat an A.K. with one of those.

I had earlier tried to get into the Nissan but the doors were locked, I thought why not, I tried the rear door. I couldn't believe my luck, it opened. Now I really was armed for bear, polar bear, bloody big bad vicious bastard type of bear! I searched the vehicle. There was a canvas satchel with ten 40mm grenade rounds and a smoke grenade. I also found a panga and an empty U.S. army plastic water bottle lying under it; I wondered how many people had been tortured and killed with that panga? I also found two small hand grenades and the holster for the S&W in the glove compartment. I went back into the shadows after closing all the doors.

I re-organised myself again. I found a way to strap the panga onto the satchel. The S&W holster went on my belt as well but cross-draw. I was ready to boogie.

I think that I was about to make a decision about what to do next when I heard a vehicle behind me which slowed down and then drove off towards Kisangani. It didn't come past me. I didn't see it. There was no turn-off. Still no sign of Y'all or the driver.

We were about ten kilometres from White Shirt's base of operations; had the driver been sent to fetch him? Whatever they were doing, I didn't have a lot of time. There was no way that I was going to get that Nissan to start. I even searched the car again for a spare key - no joy. I'd have to backtrack that phantom vehicle; I was sure that it had been up to no good. I couldn't leave the Nissan; I had to destroy it.

I wasn't going to waste any of my new found toys, and besides I didn't want Y'all to know that I had found the M 79; after all, it should have been completely hidden under the carpet. I was going to burn the Nissan. I disconnected the fuel line, emptying the surplus into one of my empty designer water bottles. I took the porn magazine, tore it up and placed the bits on the two front seats. The diesel and the brandy were poured onto the paper and seats and then lit. It made a spectacular bonfire. I walked away in the direction that the phantom vehicle had come from.

The Nissan made a loud bang when the tank exploded - I didn't expect that. Shame really, that Patrol was a nice car. Still Y'all was on foot and couldn't do anything before the next morning unless he followed me, and I doubted that he would do that. He was no fool and probably guessed that he may die if he followed me alone; the driver was going to be of no help except to track me. And if he had any sense, he was going to go in the wrong direction and Y'all was probably aware of that too. He would need re-enforcements, which meant going back to white shirt's base.

I realised that I had changed. I don't think that I liked what I was becoming, but if I was to survive, I had to allow the metamorphosis to happen.

In the last two weeks, I had started off as a wimp in Uganda, been tortured for ten days, on and off, fucked about by the Foreign Office, escaped and killed two goons as well as beating up an official driver. I was armed and I was not going to take shit from anybody any more!

I found the track; very clever. The main track passed over a piece of solid rock. A side track joined the main track at that point. There was no sign to indicate the side track as it was hidden from view of anybody on the main track. I bet that not one of the goons was aware of its existence. The only way to be aware of this turn-off would be to know the area extremely well, be an expert tracker and come across the turn-off by accident or to use satellite imagery or aerial photos.

I now was about two Kilometres from the burnt out Nissan/ambush site. I stopped and waited in shaded cover. I wanted to see if anybody was following or tracking me. I'd been walking for over an hour but I had been trying to leave no discernible trail. I needed the rest and time to think. I also needed a drink; I wished that I had kept some of that brandy, but then again I needed a clear head. I drank one of my half litres of designer water. I was down to one and a half litres, with two empty half litre fragile bottles in the satchel.

I had been lucky. The goons had been careless. They wouldn't make the same mistakes in future. I looked around. The ground was generally rising, and the soil was getting poorer. The vegetation was getting a lot thinner and changing. Cover was getting sparser. I couldn't stay here long; I had to get going but I also had to know if I was being followed. I also needed to rest; I was still severely bruised and suffering shock from Y'all's hospitality and from just killing two human beings.

At the same time, I knew I had to keep my act together if I was going to survive. However, I did allow myself a pat on the back for what I had achieved. Stop it, don't get cocky, that is the road to disaster - stay afraid, be paranoid if you want to survive!

I stayed another half hour, but still nothing. Y'all and the driver were being very careful or on their way to White Shirt. Don't underestimate your enemy but I thought that Y'all was too arrogant to be that careful, but he was not going to underestimate me again. For all I knew he was going to be in big, big shit with the President; that is if the President knew what was going on, which I doubted.

I started walking again. It was starting to get dark. I kept on going for as long as I could, until darkness completely closed in. I rested for about four hours until the moon rose. It was a nice crescent moon but enough to see by so I continued along the track until almost dawn. Jeez, was I buggered? Torture and working in a design office does not make you fit! I moved about a hundred meters away from the road, but with a good view of it from behind cover. You see, I was learning.

I woke up. I had fallen asleep; an unforgivable sin under the circumstances. It was eight o'clock. If Y'all had access to an aircraft, I probably still had another hour's grace. It would have to fly from Kisangani, pick up Y'all or White Shirt, and then start the search. Yeah, about nine o'clock over the ambush site. God, I hoped that he didn't have access to a chopper. If the whole operation was unofficial, he probably won't dare to involve the air force. I really hoped that it wasn't official.

I checked behind again. It was clear. I got up and moved off, keeping to cover as much as possible. I had to be beware of people following me and phantom drivers coming both ways. Life was getting complicated. I was getting hungry but I told myself that I could have one of those sweet biscuits later on. It is amazing how boring it is when one says the same thing to oneself for a hour. Then I stopped and couldn't believe my eyes.

Again, I looked. Since I had been in Africa, I had seen a lot of unbelievable things. But this one took the biscuit.

There appeared to be a shining, glittering pond. Out of the middle grew the biggest tree that I had ever seen which cast a shadow like a huge umbrella. Floating on this glittering pond was a brilliant white table surrounded by six equally brilliant chairs. The table was covered with place settings, just ready for a dinner party. And sitting at one end of the table, sat a brunette is a black dress, as if waiting for me to arrive.

She stood up. She was wearing one of those little black party numbers that all women seem to have. She was wearing black high heels. She adjusted one of the place settings and then sat down at the other end of the table. This was a latter-day Mad Hatter's Tea Party.

This was not real; this must be a mirage. Was I going mad; too much stress? I looked again, I had moved, something had changed; the pond was glazed or mica sandstone reflecting in the light. The furniture was that white plastic garden or camping furniture you get in garden centres. But the woman still wore that little black number and high heels. All this in the middle of Africa? That white furniture would be a dead give away from the air; yeah, me dead.

I slowly walked round until she would see me when she turned her head. I stood still. Finally, she did turn her head. She stared, shook her head and looked again. She cleared her throat, "Do you think that you could help me please?" in a very soft and refined American accent. That's me, the white knight. Oh, no, another wench who would look fabulous in a plastic bin liner; this was all I needed. I had enough problems looking after myself without having to look after a pair of high heels. Well, at least she wasn't a blonde!

My hormones got the better of me and I went and sat down. She looked at me again and said, "I was left by the side of the road yesterday evening, just as you see me. I don't suppose that you have any spare water and perhaps something to eat?" She really was bloody polite. She must have been desperate but she really kept her act together; I admired that. She must have been terrified of me. My Out of Africa gear was filthy. I was carrying a dirty satchel and of course, the grenade launcher. My safari jacket pockets were bulging and I must have stank. Oh, and I was unshaven and I had bruises covering my face. My right hand had gone that delightful clashing mixture of yellow and purple. Definitely not how to impress a sexy girl at this breakfast party. She didn't refer to my lack of refinement at all.

I had been promising myself breakfast for an hour, so I got out my two packets of airline biscuits, gave her one and the remaining half litre bottle of water. I still had one litre in my military water bottle. I only let her drink half her bottle of water with her biscuits while she told me her story.

Her name was Tiffany and she was the daughter of an eminent American Lawyer. Very rich, but then all lawyers are rich. Well they are, compared to me.

She had been doing Kenya and the Masai Mara to get over a bad two year marriage and an even worse divorce - he had married for money, a failed musician; she for love, an idiot fan, when she was kidnapped by the phantom drivers. This explained her attire. Oh, boy, another bunch of bad guys. They eventually took her to a house further up the track. That explained the phantom driver.

It appeared that the house was owned by a pair of elderly Belgian artists. The phantoms had taken it over as a safe house. They were three men and a women. They hadn't harmed her but had kept her under constant surveillance until about two weeks previously. Then they kept her locked up. Kind of co-incidental, that timing, I thought. On the morning after they locked her up, she noticed that the phantoms were very edgy and a bloody shirt thrown into a corner. Then they calmed down after a couple of days. Then the day before I found her, they became very edgy again. Coincidence again? They drove out to where I found her, and dumped her with the dinner set but with no food or water and said that they would be back shortly; and then they departed. Very strange.

She really maintained her cool. She must have been dying to know my story but she didn't ask a thing; and I wasn't going to say a thing until I checked out her story. The metamorphosis was coming along well.

We needed to get away from this place. We both needed some decent food and somewhere to hide. It had to be the house up the track. I knew that the phantoms would be back, but there was no way that I was going back to Y'all until I had a plan and more information.

We started walking, and it was hell for her in those high heels but she didn't complain once.

CHAPTER 5

Alphonse & Albert

Those bloody high heels. I got Tiffany to take them off to see if I could chop the heels down. Not a chance; they were ultra high tech, unbreakable metal/composite things.

I wasn't about to give her my boots, anyway her feet were too small, and I needed them if we got into a firefight. I was also too weak to carry her, but I could support her, when necessary. There were far too many thorns on the ground for her to walk barefoot, so she suffered.

Still it wasn't bad for me. She had one of those natural wiggles that make you bite your knuckles. The phantoms hadn't touched her; they couldn't be human. Anyway, enough of the MCP stuff. She suffered and didn't complain once. That girl had balls of steel. More guts than I could ever hope to have.

It took us about four hours to travel the about eight kilometres to the house. By that time we had no water left and we were both bloody hungry and thirsty. However I wasn't about to just walk in without doing a recce. I left her in some bushes and did a sneaky beaky. It took me about forty five minutes to get up to the place and check that there were two elderly white guys and an elderly Congolese who seemed to be doing all the work. That figured; colonial Africa, revisited. I went back and got her.

Big hullabaloo when the three of them saw us. I was introduced. Yes, they were Alphonse and Albert, with the Congolese being called Fred. Yes, a French speaking Congolese called Fred. Alphonse and Albert thought it very funny, so did Fred, but no-one could pronounce Fred's real name, except Fred, of course. "So you want food?" Silly question, of course we wanted food. "How are you my dear? you poor, poor thing."

The first thing I did was to get those high heels off her. Her feet were a mess. I would have been crying with the pain, but not her. Not until she sat down. I said she had guts.

I went into the loo and washed my feet and socks in the basin. I wanted to be able to run away if I had to. I was no use to anybody if I couldn't move. Alphonse, or was it Albert, started fussing over her feet. To be fair, he did a professional job, but then he had been a nurse before he had fallen in love with Albert, or was it Alphonse, and both had become artists. I came back and sat down. I must have drunk two litres of water and the same again of coffee and I think Tiffany did even better than me.

They were really nice people and it was a real shame that they had become involved in this whole thing. I now had four helpless people to look after, five if you include myself; my metamorphosis was regressing.

Tiffany and I took it in turn to have a shower, luxury, with me going first me first. It wouldn't be until later that I found out how lucky I was. I wanted to be ready to move before trouble arrived; and then we had lunch. I then started to get more information and things started to fall into place.

About a month before our arrival, two men arrived. They were American, or appeared American. They were very quiet, but very dangerous, much more professional than the later arrivals. They stayed a week and then left just after dark.

Later that night,, three men and a woman arrived at the house, Tiffany was with them. It appeared that the woman was the boss but that she was under orders of someone else. She and one of the men were French. After all, any French speaking Belgian can sniff out any Frenchman. It was the artist's impression that the man was from the Union Corse, but that the woman was very educated and they somehow got the impression that she was from Paris. One of them thought that she may have been some sort of Governmental employee gone bad. Of the other two members, one man was definitely Russian and the other seemed American but Alphonse said that somehow he seemed Israeli.

On the night before I woke up in the round hut, they had locked everyone up and left. They returned at about midnight, very shaken up. Fred said that he had been unlocked to cook for them and that the group were talking about the wrong man, where did he get to and where was the right one. They also kept on asking where the stuff was. They got very angry when they discussed the two American bastards who had double crossed them. What was the point in killing all the witnesses when there was nothing to hide?

None of these people I was talking to were stupid, Fred especially. I was wrong in my attitude to this social arrangement. He was as much an equal as the other two. He kept house while the other two earned money from their work. Anyway, I thought it only fair to tell all four about my holiday in Zaire. It turned out that Albert was the ex nurse and said that after lunch he would start treating my bruises. He had said nothing before because he wasn't sure if I was just another phantom.

Between us, we were able put together that was Tiffany was a minor player in all this. The group of four were Israeli based gangsters; thugs with delusions of grandeur, who were prepared to work for anyone. To a thug, the woman appeared to be a high class criminal, but to any high class criminal, she was just a thug. They were all possibly Israeli, but that was irrelevant, the secret of their success was that they originally came from other countries and were not obviously a group. Our best guess was that they kidnapped Tiffany as an insurance policy if the main job went wrong. At least they could get some money out of her father. If the job went well, they would just kill her. She was bloody lucky that it all went wrong or she would have now been dead.

The Americans were an unknown quantity, American, Israeli with American accents, Russian ex K.G.B., we didn't know. Were they secret service, using the phantoms to stop the stuff or were they organised crime, or independent criminals? We didn't know that either. We guessed that Y'all was in charge of receiving the stuff on behalf of a faction in the Zairean Government. But then, one hand didn't know what the other was up to; and Mobuto was not always kept fully informed. We knew from the discussions in the house the night before the ambush, that the stuff had arrived by road in Zaire. We also knew that a third party had taken the stuff before it reached the Ambush point but we didn't know if it was the two Americans or some other party. Was the stuff still in Zaire? We didn't know. There was an awful lot that we didn't know.

We did know that I was the wrong man. Thinking about the time when I left the Sheraton in Kampala, there was a man with similar features and colouration to myself, also waiting for transport, and he was also untanned like myself. He was a bit heavier than me and wore a temperate zone suit; I thought that he look bloody uncomfortable, maybe it was fear, not the heat. We had had an argument about our hire cars. I had been given the wrong transport, got ambushed and crawled away in my drugged stupor. It was intended that he be kidnapped to ensure his co-operation in supplying his expertise.

I remembered what that shithead from the Consulate said, "If you don't know, you don't need to know." Of course, they didn't know either, but if they guessed anything, it was that the Government had lost something and that I was a suspect. However, neither the stolen goods nor I were important compared to the trade deal. I was a sacrificial lamb if it meant getting that deal. I wonder who had shares or an offer of a directorship in the dealing company on retirement. How short sighted or morally corrupt can you get? Especially if the stuff was a weapon of mass destruction.

Someone or some people must be on the inside if the ambushers and robbers knew the route of the Presidential vehicle, which would have been a very well kept secret. It had to be White Shirt or Y'all. I reckoned that it was White Shirt because he only tortured me for a couple or hours, just for appearance's sake. Also Y'all had too much to lose if he was found out, and he was probably already stinking rich and the risk would have been too great for the reward. I couldn't see him threatening an American city with the stuff. No, it had to be White Shirt. If we could work it out, then Y'all had probably also worked it out.

Finally, Tiffany was worth something to the four phantoms alive, but no-one else was. However, she was a witness, indirectly to the two Americans, so she was probably on their death list, if they knew about her. Alphonse, Albert and Fred would be killed when their usefulness was over, and I was probably on everybody's hit list.

So what were we going to do? Waiting for someone to turn up and kill us was not an option. I was getting very decisive.

Walking to Uganda wasn't an option either. Firstly, we couldn't make it, and secondly, Alphonse, Albert and Fred didn't want to leave Zaire. We could go to the authorities, but who would believe any of us and we would probably come across one of Y'all's goons, at some time or other, which would be our death warrants. Albert, Alphonse and Fred could probably vanish for a period of time and return when everything cooled down, but if this was the plan, Tiffany and I would have to get out of the country, and we had no transport. Also, Tiffany was in no state to travel in Africa until her feet healed.

We had no communications with the outside world, not even a telephone and no transport that I knew of; the phantoms had smashed up the old truck that the three old men used. Although we had no communications or transport, the phantoms had both in the form of one of the then new satellite phones and 4 x 4 estate car, respectively. Then Fred dropped the bombshell; there was an old motorbike in a shed at the back of the house.

He thought that he could fix it up. In no way can I be considered a mechanical engineer, Albert was a nurse before becoming an artist, Alphonse had always been an artist. Well, Tiffany was Tiffany; she admitted to majoring in history and minoring in human geography and psychology and then working as a P.A. before becoming a very unhappy socially correct wife. Fred reckoned that we were all a liability and that he would prefer to work alone, so we left him to it.

I believed that someone was going to return. I didn't want to be unprepared and having the other four here was not to our advantage. "Is there anywhere where we can hide around here?" I asked expecting a negative reply.

"Yes, there's a cottage about two kilometres away up a footpath. It has no electricity but is otherwise comfortable. We can all move up there." Albert replied.

Alphonse continued, "It is in a small valley surrounded by trees; it's out of sight." I reckoned it was therefore probably quite safe. I got everyone packing anything of any use. I was now a leader of men, and woman. By the time everything was packed, it was getting dark. Just after that, the motorbike fired up, then stalled. Fred came in smiling. All he needed was something that he could find tomorrow morning, and it would work just fine.

I really wanted to leave that night, but it wasn't feasible. I compromised. We would have supper after everybody prepared some form of escape kit, including better clothing for Tiffany, which turned out to be a one piece overall, the only thing that fitted her, and some old gym shoes, she had the same size feet as Fred. I would spent the night about a kilometre down the track towards the main road, and if anything came up the track, I would blow it to smithereens with the M 79. Everybody would then make their own way to the cottage. We all knew where to find the footpath. Supper was delicious, but then anything would have been delicious after the food that I had been eating for the last two weeks.

Well, I had a lousy night. It wasn't squadrons but bloody wings of mosquitoes, and it was the dry season. In the morning, I found a marshy area about a hundred meters from my ambush point. At breakfast, I looked like a mime artist, with all the stuff Albert put on my face to stop the itching. Still, it worked. Fred was as good as his word, and by eight o'clock, the bike was running like a sewing machine. Mind you, none of them could ride the bloody thing. By half past eleven, just about every thing and everybody, except Fred and myself were at the cottage. Just before we left, he asked me to come to another shed at the back. He didn't know if the contents would be any use.

We had to walk about a hundred meters to what looked like an old outside privy. It was out of sight of the house. He opened a door which led down some stairs to a room which was really chilly. He said that we must only use a torch, O.K. we did. I looked around. There were a few boxes which I opened. "Is any of this useful to us?" he asked. Was it hell? I looked at him in amazement at the stupidity of the question.

Then I realised that he really didn't know. I can fight a defensive action against a platoon with this lot, all by myself. There was an old .303 with a telescopic sight and one hundred and fifty rounds. A leather case held a brace of side by side shotguns with an unknown quantity of cartridges in a wooden box next to it.

There were rolls of twisted electrical cable and boxes of electrical detonators, and finally wooden boxes filled with primers and dynamite, both of which were sweating but only a little bit. I looked around to see if there was any slow fuse, normal detonators or det cord, but there wasn't. Still I could hardly complain. It took us no time at all to take the stores contents up in to the sunlight and inspect it. The explosive seemed sensitive but manageable, and there was lots of cable. I also found a carry bag for the .303. That got strapped onto the bike, straight away.

It may sound selfish of me to take all the firearms, but no-one else knew anything about them. However, the shotguns would do fine for the others; if only there were more. A five minute lecture and a few rounds each showed the potential of them and they were well received. I also gave them the two hand grenades and the smoke grenade. I found some rocks of equal weight and got them throwing them. They soon found out the limitations of grenades; but it was more fire power for them.

I then got them digging holes. I was going to mine the path up to the cottage. I laid out the wire and made up twin sets of detonators and primers which I taped into plastic bags. I filled small boxes with the dynamite and set up twin and triple charges, on the likely approach to the cottage. Whilst Albert and Alphonse were digging near the cottage, Fred and I were digging along the approach road to the house.

There were two working electrical discharge boxes, huge and heavy with the plunger, just like in the old cowboy movies, I set up one firing point in the cottage and the other overlooking the approach to the house, near where I had spent that night. I set up markers. If the worst came to the worst, all they had to do was to pull up the plunger and then push it down again - Boom!

I wasn't looking forward to defusing those mines if nothing happened; that dynamite was going to sweat like a pig in the heat, and those boxes were going to be awash in nitroglycerine, still, that was going to be in the future. Maybe I'd blow them up anyway, just for the hell of it.

I was hungry and I was buggered. We had lunch late. I had a cold shower; they had a tank and shower but the stove had not been on long enough to heat the water. That's what Tiffany had said but I think that she had just used up all the hot water. She said that she hadn't but her hair was still wet. I think that she was ashamed of herself, because she wasn't able to help with the digging, and then she forgot that we needed to wash too. Tiffany had cooked lunch. She comes from a wealthy family; why hadn't they sent her on a cordon blue course? No more of her food until she learned to cook, it was almost as bad as the stuff they served in the dungeon. Almost, but not quite.

I took the opportunity to zero the .303. It was a P-14, a British design, based on the Mauser action with a five round magazine and manufactured in the States, where they put a decent length butt on the thing; and it was accurate especially with the old brass scope that came with it. I couldn't believe it, I was getting two inch groupings at over three hundred yards and I'm a lousy rifle shot. The sight was graduated in yards, but I could live with that. I estimated in meters, added ten percent and then a little bit and called it yards. I then measured distances and put out ranging markers. It was getting too dark to that on the approaches to the house. I would do that the next day. I reckoned that we had achieved a hell of a lot that day; I was satisfied. At least the cottage was as prepared as we could make it.

I wanted to visit White Shirt but I hadn't slept the previous night and I needed the rest. If nothing happened I would visit him the following night. Maybe the metamorphosis wasn't regressing.

CHAPTER 6

One prisoner & Two Interrogations

Much to my surprise, nothing happened that night. I slept like a baby. I woke up and remembered not to eat Tiffany's cooking. I also remembered what I would do that night. Stupid idea, the metamorphosis was regressing again. There was a depressing start to breakfast; Alphonse, Albert and I suddenly realise that Tiffany was in the kitchen. We suddenly didn't feel hungry any more. Fred came in and looked at our faces and burst out laughing. He told us not to worry as he had made the coffee and he was supervising Tiffany's every move.

We now knew that Tiffany could not only cook water, but also eggs and toast. I don't eat bacon, pork disagrees with me, anyway I like pigs, they are a lot more intelligent than dogs and we don't eat dogs, well most of us don't. Anyway, were was I? Rambling on, oh yes, even if I ate bacon, I wouldn't have eaten that; it was charcoal swimming in grease. Fred must have been supervising from a hundred meters away. Well, it turned out that he was in the loo at the time.

I knew that I had to put in ranging marks and caches of two stroke fuel for the motor bike on the approaches to the house, but I had found some sewing machine oil, and I was going to clean all the weapons. I had to improvise a pull through, but two hours later all the weapons were in tip top shape.

I suddenly wondered where I had put the plastic airline cutlery which I had stolen from the plane. I had lost the bloody things without realising it. This re-taught me a lesson, look after your kit! I felt such a fool, but it made me wake up; where was Albert? The other three, I could see coming and going. I was informed that he shouldn't be long, he had just went down to the main house to get some onions out of the vegetable garden. Oh shit, oh shit, oh shit; just because we had heard nothing, and that's why we chose this place, doesn't mean that there was nothing out there. I was told to stop being so paranoid. But paranoid keeps you alive!

I decided that I would take a wander down. I felt that the P-14 would be better suited to the task and left the M 79 behind. I pocketed an extra twenty five rounds and went hunting. Just as I was about to pass the last turning on the track before the main house, I took to the bushes. Be paranoid? I was ultra paranoid, and just as well. A Toyota Hilux double cab pick-up was parked in front of the house. Right, there was supposed to be four of them, and the woman was the most ruthless and dangerous, but what if there were more?

I got to within about a hundred and fifty meters of the house and started to use the scope. Just as well that I had brought the rifle. I was beginning to be lucky, and all the best soldiers are lucky, but they make their own luck. Well, I had made my luck by deciding on the rifle, but was Albert going to be lucky as well? And, could I make those phantoms unlucky?

I wanted that vehicle and the satellite phone, if they had it with them.

I watched and waited and waited and watched. I moved to the other side of the house and repeated the process, but I was a lot nearer. There were only two men, and Albert was not in the garden. Was he in hiding or was he captured? I couldn't tell. Yes I could. The two phantoms were standing in the porch but I could smell cooking. Albert was cooking for them. Pity it wasn't Tiffany, they'd die of food poisoning and I wouldn't have to risk my life. Now what was I going to do? They had made no effort to hide the vehicle or to keep out of sight.

Were they in league with someone in authority, viz. was White Shirt still on the loose? Or, were they just plain stupid? They both had snubbies in shoulder holsters, and one of them was playing with his revolver. He was pretending to be about to shoot the other one. The second one dashed indoors and came out again with what looked remarkably like an Uzi, and then pointed it at the first one.

Albert called to tell them that food was ready. They were just plain stupid and then they made their own bad luck. The phantom with the Uzi dropped it onto a chair on the porch and went in to eat. The other one followed.

You must take your opportunities when offered. I took mine.

I put the rifle down and put the twenty five extra rounds next to it. I thought that if I messed up, I didn't want them to know that I'd got a rifle. A heavy bolt action rifle like the P-14 is not so good when you're fighting indoors; why do you think that the S.A.S use pistols for house clearing? Anyway, I was not the S.A.S., so I picked up the Uzi on the way in. Yes, plain stupid; the Uzi was cocked and set on fully automatic and they were playing with it. The Uzi is a great weapon, very reliable and easy to use, but it has a tendency to go off if dropped. This one was a Mini-Uzi, even better than the standard military issue. I know because I used to read the magazines; but that was in the days when Her Majesty's Government allowed you to read about such matters.

I checked the magazine; it was a twenty five capacity job and was more or less full, and I set the safety to semi-auto. I didn't want to spray bullets everywhere and shoot Albert by mistake. I also remembered that when I was in the T.A., if there were small numbers of soldiers on the range, we would allow the Stirling SMGs to be fired fully auto at a range of about five meters. This was to show how totally bloody useless fully auto fire was; nobody, including myself could hit a damn thing. We were lucky to get four or five hits out of a full magazine.

I sneaked in. Albert was chopping onions using the biggest kitchen knife that I have ever seen. The two phantoms were drinking beer and eating at the kitchen table, but not for long. I must have made an impression because I really held their attention. They were most attentive and obedient. A shame really as I didn't really know what I was going to do with them. Yes I did, I was going to question them. I knew that there must be a set of pliers somewhere, even if only to slap in the palm of my left hand!

But first things first. Disarm them. As they were sitting at opposite ends of the table, I stood behind one of them, with Albert behind me out of the line of fire. I set the safety to fully auto and made Albert point it at the second phantom. He knew that at a range of two meters he would be cut to pieces, because he had seen it at the movies.

I tied the first one to a chair. He was entitle to some dignity, after all, they hadn't raped Tiffany or hurt the others. I repeated the process with the second phantom, and then I examined their stuff. They were scared shitless with Albert pointing that piece of bad news black steel at them.

I couldn't believe it. These guys were wearing tropical suits and had briefcases but no other luggage. I searched the Hilux, and found four full twenty five litre fuel cans in the back, but no satellite transmitter. That was understandable; their boss probably didn't trust them with it - I wouldn't.

I then searched the briefcases. They had no spare magazine for the Uzi but they did have a half empty box of fifty rounds for it. The other suitcase held a Skorpion in .32 A.C.P.. That had a total of two twenty round magazines and a spare box of twenty five rounds. These guys were not planning to go to war.

They had both got nine fifty dollar bills and a passport. I was hoping that one of their passports photos may have been sufficiently like me to enable me to use it, if necessary; no chance. They had nothing else in the briefcases except a couple of porno magazines and a bottle of brandy. Are porno mags and brandy standard issue to all goons? I looked at the snubbies. One was a really nicely cut down S&W model 10. I checked the ammunition inside, and it was fine.

I swapped it with the snubby that I was carrying. I preferred the idea of six shots to five. The other snubby was also six shot but in .32. I couldn't believe it, what was a big bruiser doing with a .32 revolver? They carried their extra ammo, one reload, in their trouser pockets; yuk, it was a mess but probably usable after cleaning with a dry cloth.

All the stuff went into the cab of the Hilux, including the kitchen knife. I removed any trace of Albert or myself; not difficult as there was nothing to hide except the onion peelings. Albert started to clean up. I stopped him; If someone else was coming by, I wanted them to think that our two prisoners had waited, had some food and then pushed off.

We blindfolded the prisoners then untied them sufficiently to get them in the back of the pick-up and drove away from the main road, picking up the .303 on the way. Albert showed me a really great spot to hide the Hilux about two kilometres away from the house and about quarter of that distance from the cottage. We then walked back to the cottage. I was really surprised just how subdued they were.

The trip back to the cottage was long and arduous due to the blindfolds, but it was worth it. By the time we reached the cottage, they were completely disorientated and thought that we had been walking for about six klicks. We didn't disillusion them. I took the Uzi off Albert and gave him one of the shotguns; he became a lot happier. I got Alphonse in to help Albert. Each of them pointed a shotgun at one prisoner. They both smiled. I wonder why?

I knew that Albert and Alphonse were happy to remain with the shotguns. They seemed scared to use anything else, but I believed that Fred and Tiffany would do just fine with the new weaponry. We couldn't actually shoot them due to the noise, but within an hour, they had got the right idea, including how to clean them. Fred got the Uzi and the .38 and Tiffany got the Skorpion and the .32. A semi-auto carbine is the easiest weapon to be taught how to use, but what they really liked were the revolvers and shoulder holsters, really cool.

I was now a lot happier about the defensive arrangement at the cottage. A complete change from the day before. Maybe Albert's capture had something to do with it. I was not too happy about the stopping power of the .32 but at least Tiffany would not find it too hard to shoot, especially with that frail physique.

We had to interrogate the prisoners. This was not going to be fun. I really didn't like the idea of being cruel, but if I had to be nasty to survive, then so be it. We separated them, tied them to chairs and everybody went quiet. Then I played a couple of tricks on them, after they had seen the pliers and we re-blindfolded them. I waited about forty five minutes before I visited the bigger one. The idiot started to sing like a bird. I was really proud of myself because I didn't need torture at all, just a hint at it.

He didn't know a lot but it was a start. His name was Igor Brazda and he wasn't a Russian, he was Czech. Our other prisoner's name was Jean Polanski, a Corsican. Igor had met Jean in the French Foreign Legion during recruit training. They had both failed, they hadn't even reached weapon training. The Legion has standards. I realised that they didn't have the self discipline to make good soldiers. They were both mindless bruisers. Jean's real name wasn't even Polanski, he'd given a false name to the Legion and kept it afterwards. He wanted to give the impression that he was on the run for a job that he had done for the Union Corse, but there's no way that they would have had him.

These two idiots met a third one, an American, Jimmy Smith, in a bar in Lyon. Reading between the lines, Jimmy was a high school drop-out whose sole claim to fame, before being recruited by their boss, was to have been sent to France to courier half a kilo of cocaine back into the States. This idiot had arrived in France and had forgotten how to reach his contact.

The three of them had tried to rob a bank security van only to find that it had finished delivering the bank notes and that it was on its way back to the depot. These idiots were found half starved in a bar in the Port Maillot district of Paris by Marie. They didn't even know Marie's surname.

Marie was a whore who worked the streets in Port Maillot, a real red light district. She was starting to lose her looks and therefore her livelihood. She decided that she was going to make enough money to retire by robbing her Johns The three idiots were her gang who robbed her victims after she had picked them up. This worked well for a couple of months until one of the Johns went to the Police; she had sensibly chosen married men.

They got to Italy without being caught where they met an old boy friend of hers who needed bruisers in Israel. He was Israeli but wanted gentiles because they would be totally reliant on him and they could easily merge with the tourists.

They started to rob tourists, and it worked because until they pulled out their guns, no-one realised that they were connected because of their different backgrounds. Marie had been in a very classy stable in her youth and had picked up how to give the impression of being educated. Her specialisation was civil servants which explained why Alphonse and Albert thought that she was an ex government employee. Maybe she was beginning to believe it herself. She easily adapted to appear to be a tour guide. Igor thought that she was really convincing, but was Igor's recommendation any recommendation at all? If all they had ever done was to rob tourists and Johns they would never have needed to fire their weapons. This would explain their poor weapon handling.

The Israeli boy friend had then been picked up by the Israeli cops; they're not awfully keen on their tourists being robbed. They were out of a job, yet again, until Marie suggested that they continue but without having to give twenty five per cent to anybody else. This went on in a blundering fashion until they tried to pull a job on two American businessmen. They had hired a minivan, Marie was to be the courier and Igor the driver, as usual. They were taking their victims to an obscure set of ruins where the other two would meet them and rob the victims. It seemed like a lot of effort just to rob two tourists, still what did I know, I was just a poor bloody scientist who had recently been conned out of his job by a scheming bitch.

Anyway, it all went wrong. When they stopped, instead of robbing the Americans, the Americans robbed them, lined them up against the wall and threatened to shoot them. But, how did they fancy making some big money in Africa? All they had to do was to rob a single vehicle of a brief case, in a deserted place. It didn't matter if they killed the occupants or not. It had all been planned and they knew exactly when and where. All the kit was ready and waiting. It didn't matter what the contents were, they would each get seventy five thousand dollars, except Marie who would get one hundred thousand because she was such a good planner; they hadn't been caught by the cops, had they?"

They left for Nairobi two days later. On arrival they were taken to a game lodge near the Masai Mara game reserve and told to wait for instructions. Three days later, the two Americans arrived took away their passports and handed over new fake ones, the Hilux double cab pick-up and a satellite phone, arranged payment of the bill for the future, gave Marie five thousand dollars for expenses and told them that they would get their instructions on the phone. The Americans then left.

Four days later they got the instructions to leave that very night and drive up to Kisangani where they would be met at the Hotel du Roi. They had three days to get there. They were to pretend to be condom salesmen and they would find a sample box under the seat, if anybody asked. There was also a map under the seat with their route, timings and petrol and rest stops marked. They were to keep to the schedule.

It was Marie's idea to kidnap Tiffany as an insurance policy. Like any good whore, Marie was a good listener and Tiffany had told Marie her story at the bar over lunch. In Marie's case it was salad; in Tiffany's, it was about three Pimms. Tiffany went straight to bed, pissed as a newt and only woke up in the pick-up when they had passed through into Uganda the next day. Tiffany was too terrified to offer any resistance and they reached the hotel on schedule.

As they started to book in, they were told that their reservations had been cancelled and were handed a message. They were to follow the route given in the message and would be met at the garage at M'eni, which was marked on their map. If nobody was there to meet them, they were to wait. They waited four hours at the garage. The Americans arrived and spoke to Marie outside the car. They took them up to the hidden turn-off where they then left them. Marie was briefed about the house and its occupants. They were told to set up the satellite phone and wait for instructions.

Igor then told me how they waited until the phone rang and were informed that they were to ambush the Land Cruiser that night and take the contents and kidnap a man whose photo they had given to Marie at the garage meeting. And that's when things started to go wrong.

Marie had also been given four metal briefcases with combination locks at the meeting. The combinations were given to them during the phone briefing. Each one held a revolver, a submachinegun and spare ammunition. Three of them held .38 Specials and an Uzi with a spare magazine, while the forth held the .32 and the Skorpion. The forth was supposed to be for Marie, but she didn't think much of .32 rounds and so gave that case to Igor. She hung onto more powerful stuff. She also kept all three spare magazines for the Uzi's.

They set up the Ambush as instructed, and the other three emptied their SMGs into the side of the vehicle; except that Igor never fired a shot. I don't think that he ever planned to kill anybody, just frighten them. Then they read the logo on the side and realised that they were in deep shit. They had killed the driver and the passenger in the front seat, both Congolese, and they found me unconscious in the back, but no suitcases or briefcases. Jean still had aspirations to be a hit man for the Union Corse and said that I should be killed.

It was Igor who got me out of the car and slapped my face until I was half conscious. I don't remember any of this but it did fit. I then staggered of into the shadows and crawled away. Meanwhile Jean and Jimmy were searching the Cruiser for the stuff When they realised that there wasn't any stuff ,Jean looked round to find me. He was so pissed off he wanted me dead, but I had vanished. Jimmy was in a hysterical state and Marie didn't care one way or the other.

They got in the Hilux and returned to the house to wait for instructions. No instructions came.

After about two weeks of waiting Marie decided that they had to get out of the country. She now started to use her brains. They had just over four thousand dollars left. She decided that she and Jimmy would fly out from Kisangani while Jean and Igor would drive out with Tiffany, and all meet up again at the game park where they would ransom Tiffany. Marie would start the arrangements by phoning Tiffany's father from Kisangani airport, making him think that the exchange would take place in Zaire.

They had to get to the airport. Jimmy was still in a state of panic as he had run out of cocaine. It was Jean's idea to leave Tiffany by the side of the track overnight. He thought that this would soften her up, and without Marie around, maybe could have some fun with her. They were going to spend the night in Kisangani, see Marie and Jean off on the plane and return for Tiffany. Igor thought that Marie had told Jean to kill all the occupants of the house. She didn't really trust Igor any more since he had not fired a shot on the night of the Ambush.

She couldn't leave Jimmy with Jean as he was totally useless. It was Igor who was to help Jean get Tiffany to Kenya.

It wasn't going to be difficult; Tiffany would do whatever she was told, as she was terrified of Jean. After they dropped Tiffany off by the side of the road, they stopped only once. It was a piss stop for the boys, Marie stayed in the car. Igor was OK so he stayed in the car with her, and this probably save his life.

As Jimmy was relieving himself, Jean emptied his Uzi into Jimmy;s back. He just threw his Uzi into the bushes and picked up Jimmy's and got back in the car. He had a cruel grin on his face, now he was a real hit man!

Igor thought that they planned to kill him as well but they didn't have the guts to do it with him knowing. They spent the night outside town in the car to save money, First thing in the morning they started to try to phone the U.S. and speak to Tiffany's father. They had forgotten the time difference and only had his office number. It was late at night when they got through and had to spend the night at a really bad flea bitten hotel.

It was decided that Marie would take a taxi to the airport, where she had already booked her flight the day before. Jean and Igor left before dawn, to return to the house but not before Marie had given them five hundred dollars each for the trip back to Kenya. They had spent a hundred dollars on fuel and the filled fuel cans which I had found in the back of the Hilux, and on beers, on the way back. Igor thought that they had been crooked but Jean seemed happy enough, and Igor was not about to argue with Jean.

They didn't find Tiffany where they had left her. They weren't worried, they reckoned that she had merely returned to the house. When they got back to the house, they found Albert in the garden. After lunch, they were going to start questioning Albert and the rest I knew.

I said that Igor was dumb. I mean he was really, really stupid but he wasn't a complete idiot. As he was telling his story, it began to dawn on him that they had been set up. There was no stuff and they were suppose to be the fall guys for some sort of operation, or at least, a smoke screen. He was weak and I didn't trust him, but he was no killer and had saved my life. I think that he would have tried his best to protect Tiffany from Jean, but now he was scared shitless of Jean, and I didn't blame him.

As he was still tied to the chair, I look off his blindfold and gave him some water. I left the door open and went into the kitchen. Alphonse and Albert were supervising Tiffany preparing a late lunch. Fred was guarding Jean very carefully. I told Alphonse to guard Igor and to take him some food, but as I didn't want him killed yet, so to make sure that Tiffany didn't cook it.

The ladylike veneer was starting to come off; she swore at me long and hard, in a way that my old troop sergeant would have been proud of, then grinned. She wasn't wearing that little black number any more. She looked really roughy-toughy in the jump suit with the shoulder holster worn in a most professional manner. And Albert was really pleased with himself; her feet were healing up fast and I could see that she no longer had bandages on her feet, only plasters and socks under the gym shoes that she was now wearing.

I was now going in to interrogate Jean. I told Fred to get out and started to slap those pliers into my left palm, with a vengeance. I looked into his eyes and it scared me. He was mad; well, that's not exactly true. He was verging on madness but was still responsible for his actions. Then I got it - a closet sadist. This was not going to be easy, or fun.

Then he just laughed at me. He stopped. He looked up and told me that he was going to kill me and there was nothing that I could do, and he'd enjoy it. He spoke in French.

Remember that I said that rule number one when a prisoner was not to piss off your captors, well, he'd pissed me off already and I hadn't yet asked him a single question.

I said nothing; I merely took those pliers and applied pressure to the first joint of the little finger of his right hand. He lasted just about as long as I did when White Shirt did the same thing to me - all of about two seconds before he was screaming. I stopped. I still said nothing. I just slapped those pliers into my left palm. Just the once, and he started talking.

I told him to speak in English. He did. His English was bad but a lot better than my schoolboy French. Schools should stop bothering to teach languages, and just teach kids how to use pliers. Everybody instantly speaks English when pliers are used properly.

It all came pouring out. He confirmed every thing that Igor had told me. I didn't have to say a word, I couldn't stop him. He was terrified of me. He had always been the inflicter of pain, never before its recipient.

It was not a pretty sight, nor smell. His bladder and bowels just opened up. I felt sickened by what I had done, but Igor's story did need confirmation and he may have had some further information.

I just walked out, leaving what I thought was a destroyed man. I walked into the kitchen, no-one was there. I found them all watching Igor. They all looked at me in horror, and Tiffany just walked out. What they hell did they expect, roses and chocolates? I went back into the kitchen to get a cup of coffee. At least Tiffany could now make decent coffee. Then I heard her scream.

CHAPTER 7

Kidnap & Mayhem

It was one of those short loud terrified screams that very quickly and very suddenly cuts off. You know, the sort of scream where the person immediately realises that if he doesn't stop screaming, he will be screaming a lot longer and a lot louder or he won't be screaming at all, because he'll be dead. That sort of scream.

That kitchen was small but I had drawn and cocked the hammer of the Browning, all in one move, before I had even reached the door. Five more strides and I was looking into the room where I had left Jean. The French windows were open and all that remained of him were two piles of cut rope and the smelly brown pool which had dribbled out the bottom of his trouser legs.

I suddenly became careful. Tiffany had been carrying that .32 in her shoulder holster, and however much I didn't fancy carrying one myself, I fancied being shot by one even less!

I quickly checked the room; nothing. Up to the French window, taking cover behind the curtain. There he was standing fifteen meters away, facing the cottage. He didn't have that .32 in his hand; he had Tiffany in his hand; and in the other, he had that bloody great kitchen knife that we had brought up from the house. It was resting quite comfortably, thank you very much, up against Tiffany's throat. All she had to do was to turn her head and she'd cut it off, all by herself.

Jean started to threaten me and told me to drop the gun. In the movies the good guy drops the gun and then persuades the bad guy to release his hostage; and the bad guy does just that - bollocks! In real life it doesn't work like that, you drop your gun and you're dead and so is the hostage soon afterwards. You keep pointing the gun at him and keep on advancing; it's the only way that works. The Israeli's found this out through bitter experience. I read it in another of those magazines that you're not allowed to read any more.

Tiffany was in real danger, but Jean thought he had complete control and that he was being the real Union Corse hard man especially since he had a knife. I still can't understand why he had made no effort to take Tiffany's revolver. I kept on telling Tiffany to relax as I advanced towards them. Fred came dashing around the corner waving his Uzi in the air. That was enough. Jean turned to face the new threat. As he did so, Tiffany relaxed. I mean really relaxed. She just slumped in a pile at his feet.

She hadn't even hit the ground before I'd double tapped him in the upper chest, two inches apart. And, all at seven meters!

All that training on the issue Browning High-Power when I was in the O.T.C. and T.A. Sappers and then fifty rounds, once a month with a club Browning at the Marylebone Rifle and Pistol Club in the City of London. It became a ritual to go an hour before the monthly Institution of Water & Environmental Management meetings. You can't do that now, of course - not allowed; at least not with a 9mm.

Tiffany was so disgusted with me for the way that I had treated Jean and so sorry about the way that he looked that she had taken that bloody great kitchen knife and cut him loose. He'd taken his opportunity and grabbed her and the knife. But she'd kept her head (partly by not moving it) and had done exactly the right thing. I told you that she'd got guts.

She got up all by herself, said sorry once, in that terribly polite voice of hers and walked into the kitchen. She sat down and only then started to shake and then cry. Albert and Aphonse started to fuss around her, but she shook her head and said, "It's all my fault."

She stood up, pulled her shoulders back, stared me straight in the eyes and said "Now I understood and you're right." Right about what?

I still don't know but you have to be gracious and formal on these occasions. So I just said, "Right" in a firm voice, smiled at her and went back to Igor.

It was Igor's turn to have a brown mess coming out of his trouser legs. It was his turn, but thankfully he hadn't yet taken it. I didn't smile at him because that would have made him even more nervous and then he would've taken his turn. I simply told him, "I've just shot Jean."

His reply was unexpected, "I think that it is the best thing for all of us, anyway he had it coming after the way that he shot Jimmy in the back." Igor was still shaken up by that, not that he really had a lot of time for Jimmy.

I realised then that Igor was the sort of man who had courage of a brawler. He'd take on any number of people, even if it meant being kicked half to death on the floor, but this type of fight with knives, guns and pliers was beyond him. He was way out of his depth. I cut him loose with a stern warning. He reply was "I haven't got anywhere to run to."

By this time everybody was back in the kitchen, popular that kitchen. They were shocked when Igor entered. He told everybody that he may as well be useful, and as he had once been a saucier in a five star hotel, he'd better do the cooking. I agreed but only on condition that he taught Tiffany how to cook. I still thought that her boiled water was suspect. Fred was concerned with his loss of function, then relieved when I told him that I needed him and his Uzi to keep an eye on the place, and anyway we had to get rid of the body as it was cluttering up the place.

He went into the kitchen and took a half empty pot of treacle and returned. We collected Jean's jacket; I insisted because it may give us away at a later date and we had no real use for it; then went out into the garden. Fred took off Jeans shoes; he could swap them in town, for good quality shoes which would fit him. We then picked up Jean and his jacket and carried him to a spot near an ant's nest about three hundred meters away. He insisted that he dig the grave because he should of been watching Jean, instead of letting Tiffany go in by herself. "Why don't you dig a shallow grave, pour the treacle over Jean and his jacket, and when the ants have had their fill, cover him over."

"It's what I was going to do." he said.

I walked back to finish that coffee that I had hardly started and he went off to find his shovel. It was starting to get dark. I hadn't had lunch nor had I put out those ranging marks or petrol caches on the approaches to the house. It had been a tiring day but I was still determined that I was going to visit White Shirt that night.

Alphonse had already cleaned up the mess left behind by Jean. Igor had Tiffany up to her elbows in flour, this was a good way to keep her mind occupied, learning to do something useful. I went off to clean the Browning for the second time that day and to check on the motor bike.

I told everyone to wake me up when supper was on the table and went to get a couple of hours sleep.

Fred woke me up at about half past eight that evening. "It's now up to the ants. Food will be ready in about five minutes. We've left it for as long as possible but the food will burn if left any longer." I wondered what was new if Tiffany was doing the cooking. Then I stopped that unfair thought when I thought of her up to her elbows in flour and how bloody well she'd reacted under pressure.

Igor really was an excellent cook. It was almost a four course meal. We were informed that it had been a joint effort, really. Everybody, except Fred, treated me like some sort of porcelain doll. I wasn't sure whether it was because they felt sorry for me, they were afraid of me, they felt guilty, they felt that I should feel guilty or what? Tiffany kept on serving me, not allowing me to serve myself, as was the habit at the house, and then the cottage. What was this, the last supper? It was all very strange.

After supper, I went and helped myself to coffee. Lots of it. The moon was starting to rise. It was time for me to get ready. As I as walking out to the bike, I reminded them to keep a sentry awake, after what had happened this morning. They just nodded. I slung the M 79 over my shoulder and left. I free wheeled the bike down the hill.

There was no evidence of occupation at the house. I checked it. I started the bike and set off towards the Kisangani road. I went a quietly as I could. I stopped in the dip just before the junction, perhaps a bit too late, but luckily, the area was clear. I didn't need to use the headlights as the moon was waxing. I headed off towards M'eni.

It was still early enough for there to be activity in the town. It did have electricity, and even a few street lights which I could see in the distance, but was obviously prone to blackouts or electricity rationing. I went past the police post before I realised it, but had not yet reached what in any other part of the world would be considered the central business district. There was even a sign to that effect, but I didn't see any difference. I turned around and went past the cop shop again and hid the bike about a hundred to a hundred and fifty meters away. Yes, the bike was well hidden from view, out of the way, but I would easily find it again.

I walked around my hiding spot to ensure that I would recognise it any direction and headed for my previous environment of incarceration. I had left the P-14 on the bike, in its bag with spare ammo in a side pouch. I was too dark to us it to any of its potential. I had brought it in the event that I was still away by dawn and needed a long range weapon. I hoped that I was being unnecessarily cautious. Long live paranoia, it keeps you alive. May be I should be more paranoid and just go home.

I knew that I couldn't do that. Someone had set me up and I was on everybody's hit list, well, that was my impression that night. Anyway, I wanted to know what was going on. I sneaky beakied up to the cop shop. The trees were well spaced apart and in the moonlight everything glowed with a silvery sheen. Tolkein would have described it to a tee, or in his case, a tree. Even the shadows were glowing, but they were glowing a darker shade of silver. The leaves underfoot crunched with every move that I made. What a waste of time, no-one cared, there was too much activity at the cop shop.

There was a truck sitting at the centre with its engine running and lights blazing. Anyone in a blue uniform was throwing kit into the back and piling in themselves. Women were wailing and kids were running around, getting in everybody's way. I noticed that the gendarmes were all carrying A.K.s. Someone's in for an unpleasant surprise tonight. Oh, God, could they be moving to attack the house? Then I heard something about an attack at Kisangani and defence, so I calmed down. They were going off to reinforce the Gendarmes in the wicked city. The local militia were going to take over.

I heard their briefing. It was in French, but I doubted that even the junior N.C.O.'s could speak French. But I could, just enough to understand. They were going to have road blocks on either side of town, a patrol marching through town and two little groups sitting in the shadows between here and the road block. All this was through fear of terrorists or rebels or some such. Someone mentioned Kabila. I'd heard the name before, but it didn't mean much at the time.

I sat down against a tree and waited. I don't think that they were being inefficient. I think that they were efficiently taking as long as possible. It looked like they were taking this call-out very seriously, and didn't want to meet the people causing the trouble.

A loud shout from where I had been interrogated and White Shirt came out and started shouting again. They moved immediately, with one poor guy running along behind and final catching up and being dragged over the tailgate. Then silence. I waited. I wanted to get my night vision back after all those headlights and I also wanted to hear and identify the natural sounds of the night.

A radio tuned to the local music station was on, so much for night sounds, but it did cover the sound of my approach. I sneaked up to what I believed to be White Shirt's office. I looked in the window. He was sitting there with two white men. They were drinking brandies and coke. The brand was the same as the bottle I had found in the briefcase that morning. Coincidence, or the local brand? I'd keep an open mind. They were talking in English. One of the white guys had an Australian accent, the other sounded Canadian.

They were bullshitting him about how wonderful the help they were getting in Zaire, and what a great joy it was to deal with Zaireans. He knew that they were bullshitting him and they knew that he knew, but this went on. This must be serious business; polite preliminaries and all that. It went on, and on, and on. Then it stopped. They started to talk seriously.

It was all about some sort of mineral concession. They were talking really big money. "Oh, don't worry, you'll get your cut. You'll also get a Green Card if you like."

White Shirt nodded, "I want a senior job in company security, with a corner office and a blonde secretary with big tits." Then he made a very rude gesture.

The Canadian nodded, "Yea, that can be arranged too." I now knew that White Shirt was not working in the best interest of his country. Well, that came as no surprise.

The Canadian continued, "You've got to keep the rebels away. Hadn't we done what we could to find the experts who were arriving to train them?" They laughed. Expert, I had been set up as an expert. I became really interested. Then they started to talk about administrative details and my concentration started to drift away. Then the subject changed again and they started to talk about women for about ten minutes and then it drifted back to business.

They had been drinking the contents of the bottle very fast and it was nearly empty. White Shirt gave a bellow and the old man who had brought me water came in. The Canadian tossed him a set of keys. White shirt spoke to him in the local dialect, the old man nodded and then left. I watched where he went.

There was a white Toyota Land Cruiser parked under a tree some twenty meters away on the other side of the hut from me, I hadn't noticed it before, it was well hidden in the open. It took some time for the old man to open the doors and then the boot. He found another bottle and closed up as best he could. He couldn't lock up so eventually he returned to the hut. He hadn't closed one of the doors properly, The inside light was still on. I decided that I would take a look. I expected to find the answers to all my questions and I found nothing.

I went back to the window, just in time. The Australian came out and closed and locked the Cruiser properly. He returned. I listened.

They started to talk about the idiot who had got away. I listened hard. No-one was interested any more. White Shirt smiled, "He's probably dead in the forest. There's nowhere for him to go, and all the border posts and airports are on the alert for him. They've strengthened patrols between M'eni and the border with Uganda, so if he's alive, he'll be caught." You have no idea what a relief it is to be considered dead.

The Canadian started to show concern about the British Embassy. White shirt continued, "Head office has said that he was merely helping us with our enquiries as he had wandered over the border into a restricted zone. He'll soon to be sent back, and anyway he was somewhat mad."

The Aussie laughed, "The British are far too interested in selling second hand London buses to Kinshasa. Those buses don't even work properly on London roads; what chance do they have on Kinshasa roads? Pommie arseholes!" My murder was going to be ignored for a deal that didn't have a hope in hell of going through!

They then started talking about the evidence, in general terms. What evidence? White shirt mentioned that his commander, he never said his name, was searching for the briefcase, and that he was a very patriotic man. I interpreted this as meaning that Y'all was so far up Mobuto's backside that he had nowhere else to go. The Australian and the Canadian didn't appear to concerned about the evidence or the briefcase. They started talking about the concession again, and they pulled out a map. I couldn't see it but I wanted it.

They started to talk about the four idiots. Now, I knew exactly who they were talking about. I thought of them as idiots as well. "We'll get the concession security guards to raid the place at midday tomorrow and dispose of those queers! Our people are better because there'll be no official record or even knowledge of what's going on." They were about to discuss the plan when two trucks drove up.

Militia started to jump out and position themselves in a defensive manner about the area. I wanted that map and I didn't care if any or all three of them got hurt. I knew that something about that concession was crucial to my survival.

It wasn't just that I wanted that map, I needed it. It wasn't just that this mine was a factor in my kidnapping, it seemed to be the root cause. These guys were indifferent to all the deaths that they were discussing. To them, it was merely part of the deal. They knew all about the phantom idiots and the house. They had ready access to satellite imagery and aerial photos, any mining house does. That map may also have been the only information that I would get which would show me how to get out of the country.

I backed off and tripped over something. I hadn't even noticed it. It was a rubbish tip with bottles and an old mattress. All I needed was fuel and I had poor quality Molotov Cocktails. I know that there was a nearby garage but they had to have a store for spare fuel or even paraffin for the lamp on site. Now where would they store it? The Militia were still marching round being very military and making a lot of noise.

I bet the store wasn't properly locked. I started looking at the doors of the rear row of huts. I was about to start looking through the windows, when I reached the second last hut in the row. Bingo! Not even a door. I found two almost empty jerry cans of petrol, a bottle of thinners and the can of paraffin. It took two journeys to get them to my rubbish tip and I started filling bottles. I had enough for four half full Molotov Cocktails. I made the wicks from the mattress and waited. Yes, the Militia were being very military, it was a shame that they stood on parade on the other side of the vehicles, still that couldn't be helped. Oops, those two bastards were about to leave.

I brought the M 79 up to my shoulder and let the Land Cruiser have it. It became an ex Land Cruiser. I lit the four wicks and threw the cocktails; one for each of the two trucks, one for white shirt's pick-up and the last one for the side of his office. There was absolute pandemonium. White shirt ran straight into the centre of the camp, the Aussie and Canadian dashed into the darkness for cover, but not before that I noticed that they were both carrying very big pistols. Where the hell had those pistols come from? where had they gone? I reloaded the M 79 and put a round into the trees on the other side of the road. I knew that I wouldn't hit anything, but I knew that it cause further confusion. The militia were shooting at everything and nothing, even each other. White shirt was grovelling on the car park, he must have realised his mistake in not following the others. He got up and ran for it.

I got up and ran as well. Not for him but into his office. I grabbed the map and dashed back into the shadows. I stuffed the map into my shirt. I hadn't done all this just to lose it. I fired one last round straight into his office; what office? I left. It took me about half an hour to get back to the bike. Partly this was due to the care I took. The shadows flickering in the flames caused phantoms but mostly, I couldn't find my hiding place because everything looked different because of those bloody flickering shadows.

Then a siren in town went off and all the lights went out as well. I could even hear shooting from the other side of town and I saw tracer. They really believed that rebels were attacking. Now I had the problem of getting out. Those standing patrols and the road block were going to be really trigger happy. Suddenly, more sirens started to go off, and then alarms from somewhere. I didn't care. I tried starting the motorbike and I couldn't hear a thing, well not at low revs.

I was about fifty meters from the road. There was still enough light to see by. The standing patrols were sitting by the side of the verge shooting at shadows down the road. I went further into the forest to get well away from their line of fire. I completely missed the road block, but I wasn't complaining. I kept to the side of the track for another kilometre and got back onto the track. Just past the burnt out Nissan, I turned off down the track. I carefully checked the house again, but nothing.

I drove up to the cottage revving enough for whoever was on sentry to recognise me and not shoot. I topped up the motorbike before going into the kitchen. They were all waiting for me to speak. They had heard the mayhem in M'eni, even from the cottage, and had guessed that I had caused it.

"Coffee, I say nothing before coffee!"

It was already made and a mug was pushed into my hand. I took out the map and looked at it. Tiffany broke the silence by demanding, "What happened?"

I sat down and took a gulp of coffee, "I've just shot up the police post. The militia are shooting at each other and at nothing at all." I continued, "The house is going to be attacked by midday tomorrow and everybody is to be killed." That got their attention, I can tell you.

Tiffany then came up to me, and just put her arms around me. Everybody started talking at once, "Shut up! We've got to move early tomorrow morning. We've got to vanish until at least after the attack is over." I let them think about it.

"Everybody goes to bed except the poor sod on sentry. Now!" I needed to think but I was too tired.

I looked at the map. It wasn't a geological map. I still didn't know what type of deposit it was, but I realised that it didn't matter. It was the money that mattered. Anyway, I was able to identify where we were and where the concession camp was. I thought that we'd pay them a little visit.

I debated causing more mayhem when the concession troops arrived or just vanishing. I'd get the others away in the morning and see what type of force was going to be used. I reckoned that after sun-up, discretion was going to be the better part of valour.

I stripped off, lay on the couch and wrapped myself in a sheet which served as my bed and was lost to the world until I woke up to a gentle kiss. I hoped that it was Tiffany kissing me; I opened my eyes, it was. My parentage and my athleticism were questioned in no uncertain terms. I was then told, "Finish your coffee and have a shower because you stink like a pig, and breakfast will soon be ready."

CHAPTER 8

An Escape & an Attack

I got up and staggered off to the bathroom to have a long hot shower and a shave. A long hot shower is worth at least a couple of hours sleep.

I had a very quick and cold long hot shower. I hadn't changed my mind because I being decent or because there was a queue. No, Tiffany had had a shower. I knew that, not because her hair was wet, but because the water was freezing. Again. At least someone had had the foresight to boil a kettle and I had hot water to shave, otherwise, I would have really carved up my face. Where were my clothes?

I went into the kitchen wearing my toga to much hilarity and comments about being the Emperor Nero sleeping as M'eni burns. Fine, but where were my clothes? Tiffany sauntered in, making comments about lords and masters and pigs being clean but not for long, then told me to go onto the veranda which we used as a dining area. My clothes had been washed and hung to dry over the chairs. They were still slightly damp but wearable. I put them on, they would soon dry. Igor brought across a pot of coffee which he put on the table and told me that when I had arrived back from M'eni, I was absolutely filthy. That figured, the 40mm grenades were powered by a black powder charges, not normal propellant, and I had stuffed the fired cartridges into my safari jacket pockets, rather than leave evidence that the attack was from inside the compound. I hoped that they thought that it was a mortar attack.

Anyway, as soon as I fell asleep, Tiffany crept in and stole my clothes, including the often almost dyed brown underpants and the socks which could walk all by themselves and washed them in a bucket. This girl had hugged me, kissed me, and had washed my dirty knickers and socks; was she setting her cap for me? I hoped not. I needed this like a hole in the head. She was the sort of girl who makes it difficult to concentrate on anything else and I now had four people to look after, and most importantly, me.

I had only recently come out of a disastrous relationship with a gorgeous siren who had screwed me over, literally. I wasn't going to fall into the same honey trap again. No, anyway she couldn't be that stupid, she was just being nice. I think that I managed to convince myself of that, or at least, pretend to convince myself of that.

I went back to where I had slept and put all the kit back into my pockets, strapped on the belt and holsters and then holstered the two handguns. It was my turn to saunter. I sauntered back into the kitchen and gave Tiffany five hundred dollars from my cache. A bloody expensive washer woman! I realised that I had been very stupid in taking all the money on my tourist trip to M'eni the night before. What if I had been caught? If anything happened to me, she may be to get out of the country with that five hundred bucks.

We had breakfast. Igor surpassed himself again, but time was getting on. We had to move, but where? Everybody had a small bag of stuff already packed, and Fred and Alphonse had packed a couple of boxes of food and camping stuff. Not much, but enough.

If the concession security guards were any good, they would not only find the cottage, they would find the pick-up. We had better make tracks, and then hide them again. I looked at the map again. It only showed the main track to Kisangani. My experience of design projects relating to the developing world was that the maps were suspect and often didn't show reality. The only reliable maps are recently produced ortho-photos, but we didn't have any of those.

We all needed to rest and to think and plan properly. Fred said that he thought that he could guide the pick-up out of the area using an old disused track that led to an old unsuccessful mine plant from the colonial period. It was very small and the investor had been conned by a prospector who had sold him the rights but to find that there was only sufficient resource to work the plant for six months. The investor had packed up and returned to Belgium, a broken man.

It was decided that the pick-up would set off as soon as possible. Once I had seen how to reach them, I would decide whether or not to watch the attack and decide if it was worth using the mines or not.

I liked making big bangs. That was a major factor in joining the T.A.. I wanted to learn how to be an explosive expert! Unfortunately, military explosive methodology is very simple and you really aren't that expert. However, I was sure that those mines would work, and I wanted to push the plunger so bad that I could taste it. Reality took control.

Oh, shit! I had forgotten to destroy the telephone cables on my way out of town. Still, the authorities probably had radios. The Aussie and Canadian must have contacted the mine that night. I bet that they didn't think that the previous night's attack was by mortars. If I was in their position, I would guess that it was the idiots wreaking revenge or a couple of rebels, stirring the shit to try and draw off troops from Kisangani. As far as they knew me, an attack like that would have been out of character.

If I were them I would put in an attack as soon as possible. We had to move, and move now! We moved.

I used the bike as a taxi, just as in the move from the house. It took about forty five minutes to move everybody and everything to the pick-up. Igor had truly become one of us. He knew that his only hope of survival lay with all of us surviving. He drove the pick-up. Fred walked in front, showing the way. I lagged behind on the bike, ready to be a hero and hold up the advance. Ha!

At that moment I had no control of events. This was getting back to situation normal for Zaire. I didn't like having my fate in the hands of others; I felt like a feather floating in the wind. Maybe this was my Karma for having shot up the police post the previous night? Then again, maybe not.

I needed to rest and think. But now, it was a matter of survival. Survive; I could rest, think, and plan later.

That track was hard going and very, very slow. It was mostly sand or covered with crumbling boulders, occasionally passing over bare rock. scrub seemed to have moved in just where the Toyota wanted to go. It should have been forest. It wasn't. It was scrubby with a scattering of grey/brown trees interspersed with clumps of golden grass. There was not that much vegetation to hold the dust down. Great if your looking for someone from the air. Everyone imagines that the Congo Basin is lush with dense tropical jungle. Well, not here. The ground appeared to be deeply weathered, but that was to be expected from the age of the terrain. There was the occasional rounded sandstone, siltstone or dolomitic outcrop. I wasn't in the mood to break off a piece of rock to find out and anyway, I didn't have a hammer.

Naturally, I could go faster than the Toyota, but it was in front and I was doing my level best to remove any trace of our tracks. So much for watching the attack. I had never done a tracking or counter tracking course, but I used my common sense. I was also really worried about an aircraft. The Hilux was a great shade of tactical white which would be seen for miles from the air. I didn't put it past the hot-shots to get an aircraft, especially after their Cruiser had been destroyed.

We reached a really thick grove of trees, or rather the pick-up had already passed through. I caught then up and made them return. I very much doubted that we would get cover like that again until we got to the old mine plant, and that was about another ten to fifteen kilometres away. We had already travelled about five to six kilometres., and if the bad guys found our tracks it wouldn't make much difference if they found us at the grove or at the plant.

I made them comfortable, set up a rota for a sentry and got them to rest. They needed rest as much as I did. I then returned down the track until I came to a point where I had a reasonable field of fire and some decent cover. It was relatively cool in the shade and I waited. I had the P-14 and the M 79. I reckoned that I had a maximum range of about three hundred meters.

If we were followed I'd take out the tracker first, and then the officer. I reckoned that despite being bloody slow with a bolt action rifle, I would have enough time to hit the officer. Officers tend to be a bit too posy to react as fast as they should; I know, I used to be one. If the patrol was led by an N.C.O., I was probably buggered. But then he would be sensible and wait for re-enforcements, which would give me time to think up some miracle.

I'd use the .303 and then if I felt that it would be of use, I'd use the M 79 but I was loathe to use it as I had only seven grenades left. I'd only use the M 79 straight away if the patrol was bunched up and I thought that I could get the whole bloody lot in one go.

I couldn't allow myself to go to sleep, so I took the opportunity to think - concurrent activity, remember?

Survive first, initiate a response later. Tactics first, strategy later.

I did an appreciation from their point of view. The attack was planned for midday, if they were on schedule. It would take a good twenty to thirty minutes to attack and clear the house. Another ten minutes to form up and move towards the cottage. They'd do that all right; they'd seen the cottage on those aerial photos. It would take them another forty five minutes to move to a forming up point and start line for the cottage attack. Perhaps another twenty minutes to do a recce before the attack, but maybe not. I reckoned that I had between one and a half and two hours to wait before they started looking for us, if they did. If nothing appeared after three hours, we would be free and clear.

I didn't think that those two bastards made many mistakes; you don't stay working on the sort of projects they worked on, if you kept on making cock-ups. They would do an air recce if they had access to a plane. Was I concealed from the air? I looked up. With the clothing that I had, and with my overhead cover, I reckoned that I was as concealed as I was going to get. Yes, the bike was also under cover. Just remember, don't look up if they fly overhead!

So much for that. What had I learnt the previous night, and how did it fit in?

Firstly, a lot of people wanted us dead. Everybody wanted me dead. Thankfully, one threat had disappeared; the four idiots no longer existed. Igor was on our side; at least for the present, and Marie was out of the country if she had any sense or wasn't otherwise involved and the other two were no more.

The secret police were after me, despite them thinking me dead. They thought that I was some sort of training expert or that I was involved in the stuff which was not stuff but some sort of blackmailing information. Who was I supposed to be blackmailing? And why? Whatever the reason, I was dead; especially since I had put an end to two of their goons.

I reckoned that Y'all was just doing his job and guarding his interests within the Mobuto Government. Why didn't he arrest White Shirt? If I knew that white shirt was bent, surely he did as well?

There were the two mining hot-shots. They worked for a company (American based because of the Green Card?) which already had a concession and had already established a presence. They were up to no good but why? They were very definitely worried about something.

And then there were the two Americans. Where did they fit in? They had arranged the whole episode involving the four idiots, and that wasn't cheap. To have developed a deception plan like that must mean that the real objective was very important to them. Were they working for the concession company as well? The two other bastards knew about the plan. I'd keep an open mind on that one. They were also ruthless bastards if they had set me up to be one of the fall guys in this mess. There appeared to be a mess up of their plans just before the ambush and I hadn't been killed, which also must have embarrassed them.

I must have dozed off because the next thing I remembered was the faint whine of powerful diesel engines, then nothing. I had at least another hour to wait if my appreciation was correct.

I heard three burst of fire over a five minute period, then it went quiet. The engines started again. The diesel engines got louder, then quieter, then nothing.

We were safe for the moment. I put my stuff back on the bike and went back to the others. They'd heard the shooting. They wanted to go back to the cottage, but I wouldn't let them. We didn't know what was back there or if anybody would return. Besides I wanted to get to the mining plant before dusk, but I also wanted to check to see what calling cards they had left behind. So we went our separate ways.

I drove back to where we had hidden the Hilux and carefully walk around; no tracks apart from ours. I saw no combat type boot prints. So far, so good.

I decided to visit the cottage first, there was more cover. I went up on foot. I went passed Jean's still open grave. No combat boot prints. The ants had been busy. They were still busy, the body was black with them, but they still had a way to go and the stench was powerful, even worse than my socks before Tiffany washed them.

I went into the cottage through a window after I had sat watching it for movement. Yes, just as I had feared, some smart arse had put a booby trap made up from an old bean can and a grenade on both of the doors. Anybody coming in the front or back door would have been blown to smithereens. Thankfully, they were No. 36 grenades, the old Mills grenade with a fuse which you knew had ignited or not. They are very user friendly, not like the new type which are bloody dangerous, even when you do it by the book. I checked all the French windows and even the loo to see if somebody had a wicked sense of humour. Just the two grenades. I couldn't see the pins, I didn't expect to, they make great key rings, so I went outside to find some one inch nails. I found some wire instead and used that to make them safe.

I found out what they had been shooting at. There was an old piece of cloth in the shed, riddled with holes. It must have been a very dangerous piece of cloth for them to have to shoot it eight times. I went on down to the main house and repeated the process.

Someone lacked imagination because they had used two grenades in exactly the same manner. More wire solved that problem. A couple of doors had been kicked in and the kitchen table had been knocked over but was about the extent of the damage.

I was about to refill the water bottle in my satchel and stopped. I checked the tank; no dead rats or strange odours. I poured some water into an unbroken glass and sniffed, then sipped it. It seemed O.K.. I filled up, and drank my fill, and then went and sat on the veranda. The two houses were largely untouched except for the booby traps. If I wanted to wipe us out, I would have destroyed both houses while clearing them. There should have been bullet holes everywhere. And how do you convince mine security guards to do house clearing?

I'm often stupid, but not a complete idiot. Tiffany! By now, her father must be screaming blue murder, especially after Marie? phone call. The State department must have been banging on Mobuto's bedroom door to get action. The U.S. believes that it has a duty to look after its citizens, unlike another country that'll remain nameless. The Aussie and Canadian must have told the official head of security at the mine that she was probably being held at the house or cottage. With the attacks the previous night, the Army and Police would not have been able to undertake any further duties so the company could earn real brownie points by freeing her and either killing or capturing the bad guys. This was Zaire so killing the bad guys would not cause any problems, indeed, everyone would probably prefer it if the kidnappers were dead. Good story!

That explained the lack of damage but not the booby traps. They would have entered the house carefully, so as not to shoot the hostage. The two hot-shots would have had at least one of their own people present to supervise and check. He'd have had to be quick and covert, so he'd have only had time for the old grenade and a baked bean tin trick. So, it was probably one, two at most.

This told me something else. The mine was guarded with normal security guards. If they had trackers, they would have certainly found and followed our spoor. If they had normal security guards and had to use a story like this, it probably meant that most of the personnel at the mine concession were normal hard working decent folk. I may be able to use that to my advantage in the future.

The bad news was that they'd know that we'd left. They said that they needed to get rid of the 'queers'. In their place I'd definitely have an aeroplane available by the next day, at the latest.

I wiped out my more obvious footprints and left. This sneaky beaky stuff was becoming almost second nature. I was well on the way to becoming a real Rambo, except I didn't have the muscles or the black sleeveless T-shirt. I'd also have to learn how to grunt properly.

By the time that I caught up with the pick-up, they had already reached the plant. They were learning too. The Toyota was parked in a shed under cover, and everybody was in the old manager's office. It was a dump but they had already started to make it acceptable. They'd even found a source of clean water. Not only that, but they had coffee and sandwiches ready and waiting for me. Well, actually they were making them for themselves and I arrived at exactly the right moment.

I told them what I had discovered and on my thoughts for the day. They thought that I was some sort of genius; Sun Tzu and Einstein rolled into one. They're both dead so I didn't fancy that much. It doesn't do to be ungracious so I shut up. Anyway, its impolite to speak with your mouth full.

Fred had been walking most of the day and Igor had been doing all the driving so I told them to get some rest. Fred was not allowed to do sentry that night; me neither but that was their orders. Tiffany, Alphonse and Albert were going to do the cooking. I hoped that Tiffany was only going to be allowed to burn the water. I was still hungry.

It was going to be a quiet night. Well, I hoped it was going to be a quiet night.

CHAPTER 9

Camping Out & Vanishing

Looking for booby traps is not your usual Sunday Afternoon hobby. I felt rung out. Still, I had taken advantage of the loo and bog paper while I was in the cottage, and then again while I was in the House. I'd even brought a couple of rolls with me. I didn't think that it was necessary as women are usually thoughtful about that sort of thing. Still, it did no harm and I now had my own roll in the satchel. I might save me from dyeing my underpants brown.

I decided that I needed to unwind a bit. Not too much or I wouldn't stay paranoid; and I needed to stay paranoid if we were to get out of this mess. The only way that Alphonse, Albert and Fred were going to be able to go back to living in the house would be if this mess were to be completely sorted out. I really didn't think that that was possible. I'd think of their future later; and besides they knew what was best for them. I certainly didn't, and still don't believe that I am the fountain of all knowledge or wisdom.

Look at me and Amanda. That's a great example of me knowing best!

I went outside and took a look around. It really was a small operation. The office block, which was really only the manager's hut, was the only suitable place for us. They had put the Toyota in the only other piece of cover. The remainder was just see through rotten shells of old buildings. Then I noticed something.

We were on the top of a shallow rise. About three kilometres away, I twice saw glinting. The only thing it could be, was the reflection of the setting sun on vehicle windows. We were not far from the track, that multi-carriage highway to and from Kisangani; La Route National, 4. Or rather, to M'eni. We were now to the east of M'eni.

That was good. At the back of my mind was the desire to see this concession. Both the concession and the Ugandan border were to the east of M'eni. So, we'd made some progress.

What was bad was that if I could see a road, people on the road could probably see us. We'd have to take real care to conceal any lights and reflections. I needed to see what the approaches were. I went to the bike and took out the P-14. The scope was the nearest thing to a set of binos that we had. I found a comfortable place in the shadows and sat down.

I was of two minds. On the one hand, it would be a doddle for us to reach the road the following day; on the other it would be a doddle for anybody else to reach us. At least in darkness, it would be considerably more difficult. However, on foot it would be easy and all they had to do was to follow the highest ground and they'd reach us.

No, we'd have to spend the night away from this place. I went back to the bike and searched around for some strips of light coloured cloth. No, none, but I did have the bog paper. I had about forty five minutes of light left.

I then heard the sound of a light aircraft in the vicinity. The sound seemed to be coming from the west, in the direction of M'eni, then it went quiet. There was no way of being positive, but my guess was that the hot-shots had done exactly what

I would have done if I were them; they'd brought in eyes in the sky.

I went back to the others and told them all the bad news. I also told them that it was unlikely that we would move before supper was over. There was much howling, moaning, whinging and gnashing of teeth. I just told them to shut up! Great management technique that - bullying, always worked on me.

They started to repack the vehicle as I rode off into the sunset. I found a hollow surrounded by trees about a kilometre away on the other side of the rise from the road. I then set off back to the plant leaving bog paper markers to guide us back. I'd follow the pick-up and remove them as we went by.

By the time I got back, the moaning had stopped. They all knew about the seriousness of the situation and recognised the sense in our late move. Still, whinging is good; I knew that their morale was good. When people stop whinging, that is the time to start worrying.

I went in and waited for them to finish preparing supper. Things were improving; Tiffany hadn't burnt the water and had made drinkable coffee. She had cut the bread without burning it and was even cooking the baked beans without setting fire to the place; I was impressed. There was hope for her yet. I told her so and got a filthy look in return. I still don't understand, I was only being friendly.

We had supper. Nothing special but it was food and we all needed it. We packed up. There wasn't a great deal of conversation. This was their first night on the run. I was an expert, I had been on the run for a whole four days. It seemed like four years. I needed sleep. We packed and moved every thing into the back of the Toyota.

They wanted to move off immediately, but I vetoed that idea. The moon had not yet risen, so if we were to drive, we'd have to use the headlights and I wasn't having that. We waited and it was a severe lesson in patience for Igor and Tiffany and they paced up and down. The rest of us sat in the car and relaxed. I relished the sensation of no real danger and no time pressure. Finally the moon had risen and it was time to go.

Igor drove again. He thought it strange that he was driving the getaway car again. 'Le plus ça change, le plus c'est la même chose.' Only this time he was on the side of the angels. The bog paper worked. It took us about twenty minutes to travel that kilometre. We turned the car around so that we only had to drive out, got the blankets out and lay on the ground. Alphonse and Albert stayed in the car with Tiffany. They thought that it would be more comfortable, more fool them. About two hours later I heard a door open and close and then a warm body wrapped in a blanket snuggled up to me and went still.

I wasn't allowed to be on sentry but I heard every movement, especially the quiet ones. I woke up about six times but went straight back to sleep.

I was awoken by the false dawn. I wrapped my blanket about the small figure next to me and went to see who was on stag. It was Alphonse. He and Albert had hatched a scheme whereby they did two hour duties in turn, letting everybody else rest. "We feel so useless, so we decided that everybody else needed the rest more than we did. That way, you could all get some sleep and we could do something useful at the same time. Besides Tiffany, the poor dear, looked so sweet snuggled up to you." I was beginning to think that they were hatching an even bigger conspiracy than the one which we were already in the middle of.

I woke everybody up just as the sun was coming up. The Toyota had no cover from the air, although well concealed from the ground. I drove the bike back to the plant and checked that we had had no visitors during the night. By the time I got back, they had all got in ready to leave. It was just as well that we left when we did, because about two minutes after we got the vehicle under cover at the plant, an aircraft started to fly over the area. It must have been the plane that got me worried the previous evening.

They looked at me like I was Madame Za Za, the greatest fortune teller of all time. The hot-shots did exactly what I would have done had I been in their shoes, recheck the area at dawn when we were asleep, had a fire going or had not considered cover from the air.

I knew that they had seen the tracks, but I didn't think that they knew exactly where we were or they would have circled us more closely. There was no way that our tracks wouldn't have shown up with the sun at that shallow angle. My only hope was that they weren't sure what type of vehicle we had. They also didn't know about the bike. Thankfully, white Toyota double cabs are common in Africa, but there weren't too many vehicles of any sort in that part of Africa.

I did another appreciation; we were about one hundred and fifty to two hundred kilometres by road from the concession, if the map was correct. The aircraft would have called up a team at dawn, if it had not already left and was on its way. Four hours driving. I reckoned that we had one hour at worst and four at most. And that bloody plane was still in the air.

I started to give orders again. That's me, Napoleon, "All right, make coffee, we all need it, and sandwiches enough for breakfast and lunch. We're leaving as soon as the plane buggers off." It stayed in the air for about another half hour and then went off to land at M'eni; possibly to fuel up but certainly to wait for the ground element.

The Toyota followed the bike. We went from outcrop to outcrop, doing our best with the tracks that we left behind. We did all the usual cowboy stuff, doubling back on ourselves and going off in false directions. I really doubted that we gained anything, but at least we tried. We reached the road and sped off east, with me in front. There was no way that I was going to eat their dust. Also I wanted to give them warning if there was trouble ahead. With the bad guys coming towards us, I reckoned we had twenty minutes before we had to get off the road.

Thankfully, the vegetation slowly started to revert back to tropical dry forest and started to get thicker and thicker. The road also started to get worse and worse. I went over the brow of a hill and saw the dust of an approaching vehicle, but not the vehicle itself, that was hidden by the trees. The Toyota caught up with me and we drove off the road about fifty meters further on. I waved them on and did my counter tracking bit, and then followed them. They were out of sight of the road. I snuck back to watch the road. I didn't want to find out that the oncoming vehicle wasn't the bad guys by bumping into the bad guys later on.

It was the bad guys. Two bloody great armoured trucks. These things had four wheels and a 'V' shaped chassis. The roof had hatches all along it and everyone had their heads out of the top. They also had commander's turrets which spouted a brace of machine guns. I later learnt that these monsters were Casspirs and were made for the South African police and intended to be used in just this type of terrain. They are the ideal anti-terrorist vehicle. And as far as the boys inside the vehicles were concerned, we were just that.

We waited half an hour just in case they had been clever, but they hadn't so we continued on our way. I knew were we were going but no-one else did; as far as they were concerned, we were running away, so after about an hour we pulled off the road in some decent cover and had a symposium.

I let everybody speak without saying a word. When they started to say the same thing for the third time I started to talk. They shut up. "There's no going back because it's too dangerous, and where would we go?" That got through. "Some of the answers lie at the concession and I think that most of the people there were probably perfectly O.K. and will help us, well, most of us. Igor and I may be a different story."

It was agreed, we would go to the mine but we would sneak in, rather than arrive in a blaze of glory.

By midday, we could see that we were coming up to the concession. The road was improving and there seemed to be signs of life. Then we topped a rise and in the valley ahead of us lay what appeared to be the mine village and offices.

CHAPTER 10

Whiskey & A Relaxing day in the forest

I hadn't really been thinking about what we would do when we reached the concession. I had been too busy riding the bike, looking for trouble coming our way and for road blocks, and trying not to think of my bum which was numb. We pulled off the road yet again. They expected immediate answers, an infallible plan. Instead they got, "Sod off!" and an even ruder gesture. I needed to stop thinking about my bum and to start thinking about what we were to do.

I told everybody to keep quiet and to start thinking and I went and lay down in some shade.

This was an established mining village with gardens, tarmac roads, a fuel station, shops etc., etc.. This place had been in existence for at least two to three years. The impression that I had from listening to that conversation in White Shirt? office was that this place had been in existence for at most a couple of months. There were women in flower pattern dresses walking around, just as they would in any village. The only difference was that the whole area was surrounded by a huge wire fence.

No! The hot-shot's company had had the concession for only a short time. They didn't say that the concession had only been worked for a short time. I had made a big but wrong assumption. This may or may not be to our advantage. People don't bring their wives to a crooked or dangerous environment in the middle of Africa. Most of these people had to be Kosher.

O.K., Mr. Brilliant, come up with a plan. As long as I had some food and fuel I was O.K.. I could get Tiffany, Fred, Albert and Alphonse in there without too much of a problem. Getting Igor and myself in would be more difficult.

I suddenly had a thought. Who had the concession before the company who the hot-shots worked for? If I was the previous owner, unless I had sold the concession, I'd be pretty pissed off. This place had had a lot of investment, both in time and money. Most especially money, big big money. The sort of money that people would kill and die for. I told myself to cool down and keep an open mind. I still had to find a way of getting everybody safe.

Albert came up to me, "I'm worried about Tiffany's feet. They're not healing as fast as they should." O.K., Tiffany, Aphonse, Albert and Fred would have tell some of the truth.

I gathered everybody around me. I did my Napoleon bit again, "Everybody except Igor and myself are going to drive into the village to ask for help. You've going to tell the truth up to the point when I arrived with Tiffany at the house. But Tiffany, you're going to say that you walked back by yourself. You all stayed at the house not knowing what was going on, and being scared of the police you waited, and when you heard the fighting in M'eni, you decided to come here for help. You're to tell them that you drove here via the plant, rather than drive through M'eni. Remember, you haven't seen Igor and I don't exist as far as you're concerned. I then became worried, "But how did you get the pick-up? Any ideas?"

Fred suggested, "Jean arrived shot up but poorly bandaged. When we found him he was almost dead. We did the best we could for him, but he died. We buried him, cleaned up the mess, heard the shooting in M'eni and then we left this morning." Brilliant; simple but convincing.

There was no way that I was going with them at this stage. Firstly we couldn't come up with another viable story which included me, and secondly, if the concession security office informed the British Consulate of my presence, the prefects would just hand me over to Y'all in the name of international trade relations.

They would be safe in the concession for the moment, and Tiffany would get her feet treated. I now doubted that the two Americans were part of this set-up and if they were, Tiffany had never actually seen them and so couldn't identify them. Albert, Alphonse and Fred were prepared to take the risk. I reckoned that in a community like this, the word would get around in about ten seconds flat, and they would just make themselves scarce for the duration, if they were around.

O.K. what to do for Igor and myself? I reckoned that Igor just wanted to go back to being a comie saucier at some restaurant or hotel. I told them to put the .38 and the Skorpion in the space under the back seat, and give Igor the Uzi and the .32.

We unloaded most of the gear and the fuel further in the forest. There was a nice secluded spot for Igor and I to set up camp overlooking the village without being seen. I moved the bike nearby. We left enough stuff in the pick-up to support their story and wished them luck.

Before they left I told them, "You must hang a towel outside a window facing our basha so I know where to find you. You must make or get hold of a map of the village and mark the security and mine manager's office. Oh, and under no condition, come looking for us. If you're going to be flown out, double the number of towels, but if you're in danger, you're to remove the towels and put out coloured markers, Tiffany's black dress will do, as if to dry. But if the towels and the dress are put out at the same time, I'll know that the dress really is being put out to dry." They left.

It took almost no time at all for the pick-up to get in through the gates and be taken to the one of two office blocks. I reckoned that this was the admin block, the other being the technical office block. Five minutes later they were all back in the pick-up with a man and drove about a hundred meters to the health centre. All health centres look the same. A large woman in a white coat started to help Tiffany out of the car, someone else came out with a wheelchair and she sat down in it.

Well, at least she was getting access to the treatment she needed. It was only being on the run which caused her feet to flare up.

After about an hour, they wheeled her into a cottage nearby, the three others, the another woman and the man followed. Fred started to open windows and hung a towel out of the window. Now I knew where they were staying. Two more men arrived after about ten minutes. The woman left after about an hour. All three men left after a further hour. All activities consistent with nurses and management helping and getting stories and facts.

There was another large single story building nearby. Shortly afterwards, all four of them, Tiffany in her new wheels, left the cottage and went into the building. The mine club? They would get food there, and that would be expected of them.

Igor and I took it in turns to watch, using the scope of the P-14. An hour later they left to return to their cottage. We waited. It started to get dark and suddenly there were street lights. I was surprised to see so few lights covering the wire. There were no gaps but it was not what I expected. The trees seemed to go right up to the wire in places, so somebody had not done his job properly. Sure, it looked pretty, but not what I would call secure. There had to be a way in, and I was going to find it. I left the P-14 and took the M 79. If there was going to be trouble, I wanted major firepower. I started my recce.

I left covert markers so that we could find our way back to the basha at night and went down the two hundred meters to the wire. Yes, I was that close, and yet I felt totally secure. I was worried that I was being overconfident but there was no way that they could see that I was there, not even with image intensifiers. I checked to see if there were cameras covering the wire, nothing, just an hourly patrol at exactly seventeen minutes past the hour. The hot-shots were not involved in overt security, they wouldn't have allowed this. I doubt if security was aware of their real jobs. I wondered what their cover was.

When it rains in Africa, it's short, sharp and deluge-like. The run-off from roofs and hardened areas is enormous. I know, I've done the calculations for civil engineers who got to go on site visits to Africa but didn't know what to do once they got there, or when they got back. I was looking for a storm drain. In Africa and other tropical areas, this is often a concrete channel, at least a meter deep. I found what I was looking for. A huge storm drain ran from the wire right up to the back of the mine club. Lots of people were now coming and going from the club. It must have been the only source of entertainment in the village apart from wife swapping and gossip.

I waited about ten meters back, in the shadows. The guards couldn't see me even if they had shone a torch in my direction. I watched the area for about half an hour and then I went back to the basha. We ate beans out of the can and stale bread, washed down with water. I briefed Igor, "You'll have the most difficult job, you'll have to wait in the shadows until I get back. If I'm being chased you're to fire the Uzi in short bursts, but only to scare the guards. If I don't return tonight, come back to the wire, tomorrow night. If I still don't get out, do what you think best. I waited until ten o'clock.

I decided that I would take the M 79 down to the wire and leave it with Igor before I crossed the wire. I would only take my two concealed handguns into the village. I would be less conspicuous. If there was shit, I would be too busy running to use a weapon, and once outside the wire I'd have the opportunity to use the firepower of the M 79 if needed. We moved off down to the storm drain.

The security patrol was right on schedule. I waited ten minutes and crawled in under the fence. I got right up to the back of the club and stood up next to the wall. I was in and nobody was aware of it. I waited until the coast was clear and started to walk towards the living quarters in the village. The art of camouflage is to appear to be what is not threatening. I was just another slightly drunk mining engineer going home to bed.

A couple of windows in what I assumed to the guest cottage were open. I chose one that was in slight shadow and climbed through. I heard a couple of voices which I didn't recognise, including a woman's voice; visitors. I looked around the room which I had chosen to break into.

It was the kitchen, why do I always end up in the kitchen? The conversations in the kitchen at parties seem to be the most interesting, so maybe that's the attraction. I found a cupboard that I could hide in if I had to and waited. I was doing a lot of waiting. I wanted to leave while there were still people in the club, otherwise I was going to have to spend the night and the next day here. Igor would be worried and maybe do something stupid, and I didn't need that.

I could hear the clinking of bottles on glasses and laughter. That woman sounded like a horse! My four heroes were telling their story like a Keystone Cops script. Absolutely brilliant! Who could fail to believe them?

At last they left. It was about half past eleven. I waited until they were well away and walked into the living room, took a glass and put a drop of whiskey into it, sat down and started to sip it. The looks on their faces! They hadn't expected me. I was now James Bond. "If it had been the slightest bit dangerous, there's no way that I would have chanced it." Their expressions told me that they didn't believe a word.

"Am I here for a social visit or are you going to give me some information?" Information.

Tiffany started, "That was the mine manager and his wife who've just left. He told us the system. The mine is supported out of South Africa and he's already informed his H.Q. of our, or rather my safe arrival. Daddy'll know soon. I told him to tell Daddy to string Marie along for as long as possible." Wise girl, anyway Marie would be receptive to this as she would be waiting for Jean and Igor to arrive with Tiffany.

She continued, "The mine doesn't have its own plane, so he said he wanted to fly me out to Kampala from Goma. Anyway, I'm welcome to stay until they can get me out. The others are also welcome to stay until the fuss in M'eni dies down."

Alphonse butted in, "The best bit of news for us is that he will arrange for the pick-up to get new registration documents in Fred's name. It'll be easier with him being a Zairean." I wasn't sure about that but I let it go. Certainly, Alphonse and Albert were known to all the key players, Fred's real name was probably unknown, or if it was known, it was lost deep in some secret police file. Maybe the mine manager did know what he was doing.

They all started to talk at once. It seems that they had met most of the senior figures, or had heard about them at dinner in the club. With new faces around, no-one was going to eat at home. This was real Miss Marple country, everybody knew everybody else's business. Just as I had expected, no-one even remotely similar to the two Americans were involved with the mine.

Tiffany took over again, "The consortium which now has the concession, took it over about five months ago. The previous owners didn't produce sufficient ore to satisfy their contract with the Government, who were thirty per cent shareholders. They broke their contract and were kicked out. Anyway, that's the story that he was told."

Fred went on, "I think that they've completely believed our story. They haven't searched the vehicle and I've still got the keys."

I replied, "Leave the weapons in the car because if they're found, you can deny all knowledge of them." That made sense to them. I went on, "Get as much information as you can about the security offices and especially the financial negotiators' quarters and office." I now wanted to leave.

Tiffany wouldn't let me go until I'd had a shower and shave. "Can I to scrub your back?" I was starting to get really worried. Just as I was about to leave by the kitchen window, Fred gave me a plastic bag. Wonderful man; it contained a whole stack of fresh rolls that he had stolen from the dinning hall. He had even included those little packs of butter and jam. Breakfast was going to be good. I left.

I stood in the light just long enough for Igor to see me if he was watching and decided that I was going to look at the admin block. No, it was locked so I walked back to the Club.

No-one noticed me. I hopped into the storm drain and out of the compound. Igor was relieved to see me make it back. He started to ask questions and I told him to shut up and then checked that the Uzi was on safe. He was relieved to give it to me. I picked up the M 79 and satchel as well and started to walk back to the basha. He seemed content to follow.

When we got back I told what the guys had told me. He was really jealous of my shower but shut up when I suggested that he go under the wire the following night to get his shower. His reaction was, "I'd rather stay dirty." But he perked up when I showed him breakfast. Fresh bread always does that to people. I didn't tell him about the whiskey, that would have really pissed him off

We woke up soon after dawn. We still had plenty of water left in the big container that we had filled at the plant. We had plenty of gas left for the camping gaz stove, so we had coffee with our bread, butter and jam. Igor looked through the cans of food that we had, "I can make some nice meals with this lot. Some of it'll be good even when cold, when we eat at night." I went looking for a water source while he was digging the hole for our latrine and inventing menus. Yes, just as I had hypothesised, a small spring half way down the hill. It was discharging about half a litre a minute, I couldn't box it but I had fun building a micro dam, big enough to make filling our smaller water container and the water bottles easy.

We sat and watched the camp for a bit. It was the usual hive of activity that you would expect from a mining village. People coming and going, but most of the men away at the mine. We then went back to taking it in turns to watch in case anything unusual happened. Igor took first watch while I used branches to make a frame which would make the latrine more comfortable to use. Believe it, or not, it was a Green Beret who taught me how to do this; the British Army doesn't consider such things.

The rest of the day was just a pleasure, sitting against a tree, watching the camp and eating Igor's cuisine.

CHAPTER 11

A Spare Shirt & a Long Trip

Igor was right, his food was bloody good even when cold. I told him, "You should go back to cooking." He agreed and said, "If I get out of this alive, I'm going to Vienna where a friend of mine can get me a job in a restaurant. I'm going to grow fat and famous and never, never be dishonest again. I don't like the class of people that you meet on the wrong side of the law." He gave me a very strange look and then burst out laughing. I decided then to see if I couldn't get him safely back to Europe. That's me, Mr. generosity. The only problem was that I didn't know how I was going to do it.

We repeated the process of the previous night. Igor waited outside the wire, near the storm channel, and I became the slightly drunk mining engineer, yet again. And yet again, I climbed in through the kitchen window. This time they were alone and waiting for me. They were all wearing new clothes and looking very pleased with themselves.

"Daddy's put money into the mine's account." Tiffany was now a little rich girl. She showed me a bundle of notes, all fifty dollar bills. She gave me half. I was now a little rich boy! They went straight into my pocket to be introduced to my other dollar bills. I was ordered to take my shave and shower while they talked; they had a lot to say, they had been very busy.

Madame started to spout forth, "The mine's got a small office in Goma, adjacent to the Rwandan border. The office manager there has already arranged the transfer of ownership documents and new licence plates for the Toyota. He's booked a flight for me on the Air Uganda flight tomorrow afternoon, but I've refused to go." Idiot woman! "Anyhow, I've no passport. She looked sheepish, 'The office manager has spoken to the American Honorary Consul and between them they've put together some documents and given gifts to the heads of immigration and of customs at the airport to let me out. Anyway I'm not going until I know that you're safe."

Bugger that! There was no way that I was going to be safe until she was out of the country and I could stop worrying about her. I could then start worrying about myself.

It's strange isn't it? You can have any number of men to look after, and you can still think about your own best interests. Just one woman, and she doesn't even had to look good in the plastic dust bin liner and you're stuffed; all you can think about is her well-being. You become the instant hero. "Bugger it! I want you out of the country so that I can find a way out myself without leaving in a body bag. You're going!"

Whinge, whinge, whinge. "O.K. I'll go, but I'm not leaving Uganda until I know that you're safe." It was agreed, the boys would drive her down in the morning, leaving at dawn, collect the documents and number plates on the car and put her on the plane.

The artists would stay for a couple of days at the mine and return to the cottage. She's given them some money as well. I remembered Igor. He still had his new fake passport. We now had money. I very much doubted that anybody was looking for Igor in Goma, so I suggested, "Can Daddy pay for Igor to fly to Vienna? He's a bloody millstone around my neck and I owe him, don't I?" Well, I'd promised myself. I piled on the moral blackmail, "Without Igor around, I'll be free to use the bike to sneak into Uganda and contact the cops there." So it was agreed. "When you leave at dawn, stop the Toyota just out of sight of the compound gate, I'll leave a marker, and pick him up. Drop him off in Goma and he can make his own way to the airport, buy his ticket and start a new life."

I now only had me to worry about. "Tiffany, phone the Mine Manager about your change of heart, and see if he can rearrange your flight." He would phone right back. He was as good as his word. Within ten minutes, he rang back. "It's all arranged, he's also organised a mine security vehicle to escort us to Goma."

I was about to get dressed when I was told to wait, and then given gifts.

I was now the owner of new underwear and a new shirt. I was also the owner of one of those hiking day packs with masses of pockets on the outside and lots of survival gear including a compass. In another bag was some oil and some rags. I could clean the guns. There was even new underwear and a shirt for Igor.

I was also given four of those five litre emergency fuel cans and four bottles of two stroke oil. Fred then gave me two kid's packs. I didn't understand. He strapped them together, and then I understood. They made a pair of saddle bags for the bike which I could just drop over the seat. I could now carry spare fuel. With a full tank and this reserve, I would get over the border on the bike.

That was all the problems solved. I was on my way to York and a quiet life! Not only had they been busy shopping but they had been busy thinking.

I packed everything up and briefed them to put Igor's guns under the seat with the others, as they may need them at the cottage, or the house.

It was time for me to leave.

To Tiffany, "I'll meet you at the Sheraton in Kampala." and was about to leave when Albert stopped me.

He said, "We went to a show in Mbarara a couple of months back; at the Lake View Hotel." It appeared that it was quite common for Zaireans to travel vast distances to get entertainment.

He continued, "The Lake View Hotel is a nice place with impressive wooden carvings in the lobby and very friendly staff. You'll be comfortable there waiting for him. If you hire a car and driver, he won't have to use the bike to travel all the way to Kampala." It was arranged.

Tiffany then said, "It's a shame that we can't use the keys."

"What keys?"

"I've got a set of master keys for the guest cottages. I told the maid a cock and bull story about having mislaid the keys to the cottage. The only spares were master keys, but the admin manager had lent her a set. "And I know which is the hot-shots' cottage. It's next door."

I walked out of the front door and straight to next door's entrance. Using the keys, I walked straight in. It was all perfectly normal except for one door which was locked. It was one of the bedrooms. I used the keys again. I could see that the blinds were drawn, strange. There were also curtains. I knew that because there were blinds and curtains in the other cottage. I bumped my way the window, closed the curtains, bumped my way back to the door, closed it and switched on the light.

Boy, oh, boy! It was a spy shop! They had all sort of electronics which was way beyond me, and best of all a whole box of passports for several nationalities. I took a look. They even had entry and exit stamps. All they needed were the photos and an entry stamp for Zaire. They even had fake stamps for Kinshasa and Goma. I was surprised to find that they didn't have a camera, but they probably didn't think that it was necessary.

I pocketed two Irish passports. They didn't have bar codes and I could pass as an Irishman, even with my accent, if I had to. I took some of the sticky covering and stole the labelled Irish press to imprint a stamp on the photo. All I would need would be a passport photo and an Irish name.

On the same desk as the box of passports, lay an open box containing passport sized photos of the hot-shots; now I knew why they thought that they didn't need a camera. I pocketed two of each hot-shot; I didn't know if they would be useful, but they weighed nothing and took up no space.

I had been so amazed by the spy kit that I hadn't even looked at the walls. I looked. There were four photos on the wall; two had circles surrounding their faces with a cross in the centre and the words, Got ya! written underneath. The other two photos were compatible with the description of the two Americans that Alphonse and Albert had given me when we had first met. I needed to think, but not that much, I was leaving the country and going home. I switched off the light and left the place otherwise as I had found it; cracking my shins again on the way out.

I didn't tell the gang about my thefts, but I did tell them about the photos on the walls. We agreed that we thought that the reason that it had all gone wrong for the Americans was that the hot-shots had bumped off two of them, and that the others were probably in fear of their lives.

I said my goodbyes, kissed Tiffany on the cheek, "I see you at the Lake View Hotel." I picked up my presents and left through the door. I sauntered off towards the club like a mining engineer who fancied his chances with the new girl. I walked around the corner straight into the security patrol.

I kept on going and made some comment about the weather, and prayed. One of them looked at me a bit strangely but no-one stopped me. This randy mining engineer bit really worked! I reached the back of the club with my new underpants almost dyed brown, yet again. I jumped into the storm drain for what I really hoped was the last time and slipped out under the fence.

Igor had almost wetted himself. Firstly the time that I had taken, and then when I had bumped into the security patrol. He was just about to fire a burst in the air when he realised that it wasn't necessary. Before he had a chance to say anything else, I told him to shut up, checked that the Uzi was on safe, gave it back to him this time, gave him the M 79 and walked back up to the hill to the basha. Igor followed, muttering quietly.

He cheered up considerably when I told him about his plane trip and the plans for the following morning.

I gave him his new clothes, which he would need before he got on the plane. There wasn't a lot that we could do to prepare him, but I put the Uzi, the .32 and his new clothes into his briefcase. I would sort out the camp after he left. We had about five hours before dawn and we weren't going to sleep because we didn't know if we would wake up in time. Anyway we had to get to the rendezvous. I left all my kit except the M 79 and satchel and we left. It took us about two hours to reach what I considered a suitable R.V.. I was perhaps over cautious but we had plenty of time and I really didn't need to screw up at this point, when I had a real chance of getting away.

I hung bog paper on a tree, just as we had arranged, and waited. First the false dawn, then the true dawn, then nothing. Oh, bugger, what had gone wrong? We waited at least another half hour and then a Land Rover came out of the compound followed by the Toyota. Just by the bog paper, the Toyota stopped. Fred leaned out his window and shouted something in a local language and the security guards just laughed. Both Alphonse and Albert got out looking to all the world as if they needed a leak. Fred drove the pick-up a little further into the trees and stopped. He had effectively blocked the guards' line of sight.

The guys had only enough time to say goodbye again and to tell me that the reason for the delay was that the guards had to fill up the Land Rover with fuel. Everybody got back into the car with Igor crouched down between Albert and Alphonse who were sitting in the back. They left. I was on my own and it was time for me to make my way back to Uganda.

There was nothing and nobody, so I re-crossed the road and made my way back to the basha. It only took me an hour. I looked around my home and started to clear up. I repacked my kit that I needed for the trip, the rest I buried less the big water container and the perishables which I put by the side of the road. I knew some family would find them useful and that they would vanish without trace.

I looked around In a couple of days, no-one would know that we had been there. I suppose that if I had been S.A.S. trained, there would of been no trace at all, but I didn't think that anybody would come looking, and it didn't matter if they did. I set off for Uganda.

It was a long trip to the border and I had to be very careful. I was loaded for bear with no documents, so if I were stopped, I was a dead man. I was careful. I spotted two road blocks and went around them. I also had to go around two small towns. I had no choice but to roar straight through at least half a dozen villages, but no-one seemed to care. I suppose they were too busy surviving to take any notice.

The first of the two big problems was identifying which metropolis was Mambasa; it has a key cross roads, and I needed to turn right towards Beni. I solve this by skirting around the right hand side of the town until I came across the Route 430.

The second major problem was Beni itself. It was also centred on a cross roads. This time I had to go straight over. It was another sixty kilometers to the border post at Kasindi. Those sixty kilometers are within the Parc national de Virunga.

As I skirted both Mambasa and Beni, I naturally got lost. Thank you Tiffany, for the compass!

Just as the sun was passing below the horizon I saw the Custom's post. There was nothing, then the border post; that's it. Around the corner and there it was. I back-tracked with extreme rapidity. I drove to the highest hill I could find and looked around. I needed some idea of the lay of the land, if I was going to cross the border undetected. There was nothing I could do, so I had something to eat, got out my blanket, lay down and slept.

I looked at my watch; it was eleven o'clock, and the sun was burning my eyes out! I had slept for a full fourteen hours, but I did feel better. I filled up the bike. I made myself some food and coffee. Not wonderful, but it went down well.

I got out the P-14 and used the scope again. It was so simple to get by. I could have done it the previous night without too much trouble. I forced myself to think. Was there anything that I must do before I left Zaire, never to return. I cleaned the weapons. It gave me something to do while I thought.

I was leaving the hot-shots and the Americans well behind. I was entering a safe country; well, as safe as any African country can be, and I was about to cross the border. And that night I was going to sleep in a bed! I had better get rid of the guns. If I got stopped by the Ugandan cops without papers, the worst that they would do is throw me out of the country. With illegal guns, I'd be in jail, don't pass Go, don't collect two hundred pounds. With one gun maybe I'd get away with it. No, I wouldn't chance it. A white man on a motor bike is obvious so I had better look as touristy as possible. I separated out the weapons, ammo, and all unnecessary kit and put it to one side with the satchel. I stopped and became paranoid again.

I looked around again. It was a conical hill, lightly but sufficiently wooded and apparently rarely visited. I could find this place again in my sleep. I looked for a suitable spot and finally killed my panga. I dug a hole. I then packed the weapons and the rest of the stuff that I didn't need into bin liners. I put the whole lot into the hole and filled it in, patted it down and covered it with stones and chucked a bit more dirt on top. I reckoned that it was pretty invisible and that I could find it again if I ever had to.

The passports and other junk went into the day pack. I cleared up any other evidence of my stay and left. I free wheeled down the hill to my escape route and started the bike at the bottom of the hill. It was as easy as I had planned. I was in Uganda! All I had to do was to get to Mbarara. I just followed the track the trunk road to Kampala, and kept to the speed limit. I was lucky, no road blocks, except for one which I saw well in advance and which I bye-passed. At about half passed five, I reached the outskirts of Mbarara.

I slowed down, but not much because the bike was dying and started looking for signs of the Lake View Hotel. Just before I came into town, on the right hand side, was a sign and turn-off. I took it and just up the road, on the left hand side was the entrance to the hotel. The bike died just as I reached the columned entrance. I walked in.

Sitting in the reception area, just before the reception desk, sat Tiffany in the presence of a rather large young woman. Tiffany got up and rushed towards me and gave me a big hug. The young woman just scowled. I could see that I had a real friend here. I was introduce, and was informed that she was from the security section of the American Embassy. That figured, I could see the butt of a rather large revolver peeking out from under her waistcoat.

I had been booked in and could I sign in. "Your passport please? And would you like a passion fruit juice?" Tiffany produced an official looking document which turned out to be temporary papers from the British High Commission. I was tired, hungry, I stank and I needed a shower. I needed a stiff drink more and I wanted to know how she had arranged all this.

She started to tell me.

CHAPTER 12

A present from America & a New Friend

She'd only started to make her first sound when I told her, "Drink first, then talk"

I smiled, "I really need a stiff drink and there has to be a bar somewhere around here. Let's go there before I collapse, and then you can start talking." Tiffany walked out of the hotel entrance and motioned us to follow her. We did. She explained, "The service is quicker at the poolside bar, and the sooner you get your drink, the sooner I can start my story." Seemed reasonable to me. Tiffany told her story.

They had long, but a totally uneventful trip to Goma, where they met the mine local office manager and the Honorary American Consul and received the papers and new number plates for the Toyota as well as Tiffany's temporary passport. The guards had not noticed that two white men had got into the car and that three had got out, so that was no problem.

The guards had to return immediately if they were to complete their journey in daylight. A tearful departure ensued and Alphonse, Albert and Fred left following the Land Rover. A taxi was found for Igor and he left. Tiffany had given him two thousand dollars to get him to Vienna, while they were still in the car.

The Honorary Consul, manager and Tiffany had lunch and then went on to the airport. She was given V.I.P. treatment. Igor was also on the plane and pretended not to recognise her, which she thought was very sensible. The Amazon scowled. She was met at the airport by someone from the consulate and taken straight to the Embassy.

It turned out that the Ambassador was an old buddy of her father's and was going to put her on the first plane to the States. Naturally, she refused and even had to stamp her feet, which must of hurt quite a bit. The amazon really scowled at this point. She told His Excellency exactly what she was going to do and exactly what had happened, sparing no details. Seeing that she was even more stubborn than her father, he realised that his only option was to help her.

He contacted the Brits, who agreed to some paperwork, as long as I saw them as soon as I arrived in Kampala. The amazon scowled again, but at me this time. He, or rather his P.A., then booked the rooms at the Lake View Hotel. He arranged her bodyguard and official car, this time the amazon smiled, and they got to the hotel about two hours before me. We were to spend the night and leave the following morning.

I ordered another drink and then told her my adventures, leaving out the bits about the guns and avoiding road blocks. I didn't think that the amazon would take too kindly to that. She asked, that is the amazon asked, some really sensible questions; this was no ordinary bodyguard. She looked at me with a little, but only a little, admiration.

The amazon started to speak, "My orders are to deliver you to the High Commission as soon as we arrive in Kampala, and I reckon that you're going to be put incommunicado until they can get you on the first flight to the U.K.. There's one tomorrow night so you're going to be on it." It sounded like her opinion of the prefects was as bad as mine. "You'd better get your story straight now and write down Tiffany's phone number while you've still got the chance." I was beginning to like my amazon.

"You stink like a pig. Go and shower before I've got to find a gas mask. I went to my room where a very respectable set of casual clothing lay on the bed. Tiffany had excellent taste. I showered and changed. I was warned that the hotel could not wash my clothing before I left the next day so I bundled it up and put into my day pack. Maybe when the prefects searched me, they wouldn't notice the passports, but then again, maybe they would. I'd better do something else. I somehow had a premonition that I'd need them sometime.

We had dinner and I went to bed early. I was awoken to a scratching at my door. I opened it, and well.... A gentleman just doesn't discuss his bedroom activities.

I woke up to my seven o'clock alarm call and kicked Tiffany out. I dashed to the shower. I was going to have my shower first, before she started her's. I knew that she was perfectly capable of using a whole hotel's supply of hot water, all by herself.

Oh, hell, what had I done? I didn't need another woman in my life. I didn't need my emotions all screwed up and when was I going to see her again, or if?

We all met for breakfast, the amazon giving us that 'I know what went on' look. Mind you, it was her job to know, and after her questions the previous day, I thought that she probably knew her job very well. We left on schedule and got into Kampala about four hours later.

I was deposited at the High Commission, having said goodbyes earlier, and whisked into a very high powered bureaucrat's office. "You're on the next plane out to London and I'm not interested in any stories that you may have to tell. You can wait in the adjoining room." It contained two easy chairs, a table with a chair on either side and that's it. I knew that there was no point in complaining so I sat down in an easy chair and dozed off.

At six, we left for Entebbe. No formalities, a minion arrived and told me to follow him. I picked up my bag and walked. It's a long trip for such a short distance, very busy. We arrived and were past through the airport road block, it being an official car. We walked into reception, my day bag being duly scanned for bombs. My minion collected my ticket and started to fill out my departure forms. He paid my twenty dollar airport tax and took me to immigration where he passed over a new set of papers with the forms. We went through to the waiting area.

He was pissed off with me because he had to see me on the plane and he had to miss a hot date. He really wasn't a bad sort. He didn't know what I had done wrong, and didn't want to know, but he looked at me as if I was a snake about to strike.

He put me on the plane like the good boy that he was, and we eventually took off.

The flight was the usual nonsense. The flight attendants were giving everybody shit and bossing them around. Do British flight attendants do a bitch course? I don't remember what the movie was, but it was so bad I found the in-flight magazine more interesting. As you can imagine, it was a fun trip.

The arrival at the mother country was just as much fun. I was informed that I was to stay on board until everybody else was off. The man from the ministry arrived and took my temporary documents. He told me, "It is your fault that the bus deal has fallen through!" Did those idiots really think that they had any chance of selling second hand buses to Zaire, well, I suppose they did. "Having a passport is a privilege and not a right, and there was no chance that you will be granted another for at least five years, if ever again!"

I bypassed immigration and was taken to the red zone at customs. They searched my bag and told me to empty my pockets. I think that they were just being nasty. The custom's guy looked sheepish. He didn't have time to be nasty on behalf of the Foreign Office; he was trying to stop the illegal importation of drugs and other nasties that ruin people's lives. I had been clever. After the amazon's warning, I had made up a parcel of the two passports, the sticky and the press and asked Tiffany to post to me at a friend's address in Surbiton. As I was passing it over, she asked, "What's all this junk?"

I grinned, "You don't want to know."

She grinned back, "You're probably right."

They kicked me out and left me to my own devices. It was raining. I took the tube and a taxi home to the flat. Me and my bag went upstairs to my front door. York, here I come. I was going to phone the York consultancy and tell them of my decision. I was still a bit paranoid and felt a tiny bit of resistance as I opened, or rather tried to open the front door. I stopped and looked down and saw the string.

The last time that I saw a bit of spring across a door was when somebody was trying to kill me. If not me, then Alphonse or Albert. The last time, I had the good fortune to be on the inside of the door.

I gently closed and locked the door and went downstairs. I needed to be sure. I went to the local corner store and bought a pair of huge scissors. I returned and gently reopened the door until I met that resistance. I took another look, yes it was string. I stood to the side of the door and put my hand round and cut the string. There was a sort of thunk sound. I crouched down and counted to ten. Nothing.

"What are you doing? from above. I looked up and saw the stupid enquiring face of a young man who had been visiting or delivering something to another flat. If what I was afraid of had happened, he would have been an ex visitor or delivery boy. I told him, "I've just come back from foreign parts and I'm feeling a bit faint."

He mumbled something about, ".....being better to stay in good old England." and departed.

I very carefully stepped through the door. There was the baked bean can on the floor. I found some wire and made the Mills bomb safe. Oh, hell, the cops wouldn't believe me. They'd just think that I was mad.

I knew that it wasn't the ministry. The prefects may have hated my guts but killing isn't their style, its too dirty. If anything nasty has to be done, the S.A.S. or S.B.S. are tasked to do the dirty deed, and I wasn't worth the trouble. Besides, this was not a professional job. It wasn't specific to me, anybody with a key to the flat could have been killed, and success wouldn't have been assured using this method.

Amanda may have hated me, but she wasn't about to kill me - she didn't hate me that much, and what for? I wasn't going to trouble her again and she had got what she needed out of me - my job. So who?

I looked at the knot in the bottom of the tin. It was the same double figure of eight knot. This was too much of a coincidence. The shot-shots or one of their minions. They were bloody quick, I had only just reached Kampala the day before; however, my body had not been found and the attack on the house and cottage had taken place five days previously. They could have sent somebody here, and booby trapped the place in case I did return.

The place was otherwise as I had left it. I took enough clothes for a week. The remaining decent clothes, I packed and put them with the two trunks of books and other valuables. I left. I went down the pub, I needed to think and the pub was a nice public place where I'd be safe for a bit.

I bought a double brandy and sat down. I took enough to steady my nerves. I now knew why bruisers had the brandy, it steadies the nerves a damn sight faster than whiskey.

I thought that it had all ended with my return but it was worse because I was totally defenceless in a defenceless society. I realised that they would always be after me, simply because I was alive. I had to fight back if I was going to survive, and without mercy. No quarter given, or taken. Then I had to vanish. A new life, but where? Doing what? I had to think.

A man sat down next to me and started to speak, "Man's been looking for you. A very nasty looking man. And I know what I'm about talking about because a very nasty man's looking for me too. I'm your postman." I looked up. Yes, he was in a postman's uniform. He was a bit older than me but looked like a body builder and he had a No.1 haircut. I looked at him more carefully. "Nasty bloke, American. Mine's an American too." He realised that I wasn't going to talk, so he continued.

"Got a girl friend. Nice girl. Been beaten up by her boy friend. I looked after her and she's moved in with me. Best thing that's ever happened to me. But the boyfriend's bad news. Mafia. Likes hurting people. Part of a new group which is taking over here, in London. They're even taking over the established Mafia. Very, very bad news. The boyfriend doesn't like his woman leaving him, makes him look bad, so he's looking for revenge."

"We need to get out of the country. I've got a mate on the Costa Brava who'll give us a job if we can get out there. Nice climate. Nice work. And safe. Problem is, I don't have a passport. She does, but she won't leave 'til I can. Trouble is, I haven't bothered to renew my passport since I left the Army." He told me his old Regiment. "Did my bit in the Falklands and four tours in Northern Ireland. Even got a couple of medals. Got promoted six times and busted six times. Trouble is, I wasn't trained for this and I'm buggered if I know what to do."

And I was the expert?

"I know that you don't know me from a bar of soap. You're always out when I delivered. I know that you're some sort of engineer so you got to have brains. The Sappers had brains, so you must, being an engineer."

Little did he know!

"Look, if you help me, I'll help you. You'll be the brains and I'll be the brawn. And we'll get both these bastards." Here was a real bloody warrior asking me, a week-end jobby for help. Still, I'd survived Zaire so maybe I did know what I was doing.

"Seen your eyes; when you'd come in. Wary, very wary. Just like some of those undercover boys in Northern Ireland. You'll know what to do."

I pulled out the pictures of the hot-shots that I still had and asked him, "Seen either of them?"

"No, but the little shit who asked about you and her ex boyfriend are the same type."

Then it occurred to me, was this postman a British official? I asked him what he wanted to drink and went to buy his beer and a top-up for my glass. I asked the barman about the postman. The barman informed me that he came in every lunchtime, had done for the last two years. I was satisfied.

I returned to the table. He congratulated me on the way that I had checked up on him, "Very professional. Done this sort of thing often?" Great, the blind leading the blind. I told him just enough to scare him, but he still thought we could help one another.

"O.K., I'll make you a deal. We'll help one another but to start with, I need a safe house."

He looked around, "I've had to move out as well, and I'm staying at a very quiet bed & breakfast, there'll be room for you there. I've finished my rounds, so after we've finished our drinks, we'll be off."

It was a nice enough place. Nothing fancy but clean and quiet. I wouldn't have guessed from the outside. I couldn't have chosen a better place. I told him about the Irish passports. I knew a lot of the boys had acquired trophies of war during the Falklands. "Do you have any, or do you know anyone who does?"

"When we returned, there was a scare on the ship and everybody on board tipped their's over the side. But I do have a couple of mates who've got collections and who owe me favours. He thought a bit, "Look, your package may be checked, it coming from foreign parts. I'll keep an eye out for it, and if I find it, I'll bring it straight over."

Bloody hell, it was starting all over again. Oh, shit! if they had booby trapped my place, maybe they'd got it in for Tiffany as well. I had to get to a phone. It took me twenty pounds to convince the landlady to let me phone the States. I got through to her father's secretary and gave my name. She knew exactly who I was. As soon as she heard the state of my voice, she stopped making pleasantries and put me straight through to Tiffany's father. He was a bit pissed off being disturbed in the middle of a very important meeting but soon stopped be pissed off and became very worried instead.

CHAPTER 13

A New Friend & New Toys

He told me, "Tiffany's still in the air but I'll arrange everything. I've got shares in a reputable security company that often does serious body guarding jobs, and what's the point in owning something if you can't use it? Fax me copies of the photos of the hot-shots. I'll try and get information on them." I asked him to enquire about the ex boyfriend. "I can't thank you enough for what you did in Zaire." Words fail me. Just as well that he didn't know that I'd done in Uganda, words would really have failed him. He asked for a contact number and rang off.

There was nothing I could do about the guys remaining in Zaire. So I stopped worrying about them and started to worry about me.

I went to a photographer and asked him to blow up the photos. It would cost me a fiver. He did it in two hours and it cost me twenty five, but that also included a set of passport photos. It was worth it because I was able to fax daddy the mug shots before the local fax agency had shut.

Whoever the financial backers of the new concession holder were, they were bumping off anybody and everybody who they thought of as a threat. It sounded too extreme to be the upper echelons of the Mafia. The Mafiosi were far too respectable to want to touch these guys. It had to be a new organisation. Anyway, if anybody could find out, it would be daddy. I hoped.

I got back to the B & B to find everybody watching the telly. There had been a new gangland killing. The Police said they had everything under control, and you could see that the situation wasn't under control. What worried me was that I was now part of the situation. What was worse was that if I went around causing mayhem and destruction as I did in Zaire, there's no way that I would get away with it in U.K.. And even if it was in self defence, with witnesses, I'd still go to jail where the bad guys could have me killed.

I had to do something so I told Postman Pat that I would be going to the laundrette to wash all my dirty gear. "No problem, I've got to go to bed early cause I've to get up at the crack of sparrow fart to start delivering letters, and I've got to look into something." and gave me a huge wink.

I took all my washing to the laundrette. All my out of Africa gear was rotten. I had no choice but to dump it. What a waste. I went back to my digs.

I didn't have anything to do and I didn't want to go out to the pub. If you don't move, you don't leave tracks. As long as I stayed in the B & B, I wouldn't be noticed. I was starting to be paranoid again, good!

I just made it to breakfast, and lingered for as long as I could without annoying the landlady. I decided that I would try and get a legal passport. Then, if you queued up you could get a passport in one working day. I had been back to the flat, dangerous but necessary, and collected all my personal documents.

I went to a solicitor and got him to store them. I took my copy of my birth certificate and went to try my luck. I thought that by going personally, I had a real chance of beating the system. Not a chance. The young woman at the counter couldn't understand it but she was not allowed to issue me with a passport. She very quietly told me, "Go to your M.P., that usually works." I thanked her and kept that for a last resort.

I returned my birth certificate to my new solicitor and went to meet Pat at the pub. He couldn't believe it, my package had already arrived. I couldn't believe it either. I expected it to take at least another two weeks. He had nicked it before it was to be inspected. It had been put on the inspection tray, purely at random. We'll open it back at our digs. We started back but stopped off at one of those photo kiosks first, so that Pat had a set of photos.

"We need some names; we need real people who've died before they've had a chance to get a passport. If anybody checks up there would be a record of our new existence."

"No problem. I know enough Irish who've had deaths in the family. I'll visit some tonight. They won't like you, not with your accent, so you had better go to the pictures, or something. After dinner, I couldn't think of something, so I went to the movies. I saw one of those comedy romances, it took my mind off things for a couple of hours. I went back to the digs and found that everybody else had gone to bed. I did the same and nearly missed breakfast again.

I went to the Marylebone Rifle & Pistol Club in the City, and put three hundred rounds on my tab. I fired fifty. I knew that the best way to get better was to fire little and often and that was my plan.

I met Pat at the pub again. "I've got a shitload of names and ages on this piece of paper. I've also set up a meet with my mate. He owes me because he thinks that I saved his life twice. He really likes guns, you'll see. He's now a bookie and club owner and stinking rich. He can afford his collection, well as long as the filth don't find out. We'll be seeing him at the club at ten o'clock. There'll be no trouble because all the bouncers are my mates from the regiment." It appeared to be one nice big happy family.

We went to see the bookie. He took one look at me and sneered at Pat, "Don't you know better, he's an officer! You can't trust him."

Pat told him, "He's my mate and we're helping each other."

The bookie took another look at me, "You go and have a drink on me while I speak to this prick." After about ten minutes, a waitress asked me to go into the bookie's office. He motioned me to sit down and asked me about my recent history. His talk with Pat had obviously changed his mind about me.

I sat down and told him some of my adventures, but when I showed him the pictures of the hot-shots, he stopped me. He ranted on a bit about their parentage and told me, "They're part of the organisation trying to take over London's gangland. I've just about got a workable arrangement with the present lot, but this new lot are going to be more trouble than I can handle. Any shit that you can stir up would help me out, so how can I be of help? But first, how are you going to help Pat?"

"I've got an Irish passport for Pat and it'll ready in the morning. I'm going help him get out of the country and into Spain."

"No." the bookie said, "I've got better contacts and I'll get Pat and the girlfriend out there. You've only got to help Pat get her out of the clutches of the boyfriend. I can't be seen to be involved in that." He thought a bit. "What do you need?"

I started to tell him but he then told me to shut up. It works every time. "I can get you an Ingrams with a silencer and a sawn off pump action shotgun. That'll do for firepower. The fun thing is that they used to belong to these American bastards. Irony ain't it? What else do you need?"

What a question! I thought for a bit. Can you get me a silenced .22 pistol?" He nodded. "I'll need a couple of motor bikes, about two hundred cc. He nodded. "An inconspicuous van which can carry the two bikes and a can of spare fuel for the bikes." He nodded again. "I'll need about ten pounds of C-4, fuses, several radio controlled detonator sets and a transmitter. He grinned.

Pat said, "If that's the case, I'll take a Sherman tank."

"No problem." then he laughed. "A key to a lock-up in Paddington will be delivered to your digs by dinner tomorrow. All the stuff will be there. It'll be in good working order. I don't expect any of it to be returned."

We left through the kitchen after we had memorised a cell phone number. We took a bus back to the digs.

I nearly missed breakfast again. There was a message near the telephone for me to phone someone and collect something. It was a firm of solicitors in the City of London, and there was a long fax for me to collect. I could see that things were soon going to be moving fast.

I filled in the chosen names on the passports glued in the photos, pressed the stamp across the corner of the photos and put the sticky covering onto the correct pages. Pat and I were now both Irishmen with passports that would pass anywhere in the world including Ireland.

I left to read my fax.

CHAPTER 14

An Interview & Bad News

I was surprised that they let me in. You needed a pin stripe suit, silk shirt and gold cufflinks just to get through the tradesmen's entrance. They expected my arrival and offered me coffee and then asked me to take a seat. A properly dressed person who was also waiting, whispered, "Not even my M.D. is offered coffee. Who the hell are you?" He looked at me in awe.

"I can see why your M.D. isn't given coffee. It's bloody awful, they'll lose his account immediately." I whispered back to my new friend, but he just shook his head and whispered, "But you've been given coffee and I've spoken to you. They won't believe me." Oh, well, little things please little minds.

The receptionist, who was obviously the Right Honourable something or other, waved me through and informed my friend, "I'm sorry but you'll have to wait as the Senior Partner has to see him first." My new friend didn't seem at all put out or surprised by this. I was.

The Senior Partner was large, fat, had grey hair and smoked a cigar. "Do you mind? Its one of my few pleasures in life." I couldn't care one way or another, this was one very powerful and competent man. Why should I mind? I wanted to read my fax.

"It's very sensitive. Tiffany's father has briefed me quite thoroughly, both about yourself and the situation. Tiffany is safe. He asked me some questions about Zaire. I replied as best as I could. I finished, "You know that there was no way that the Zaireans have any intention of buying buses."

He said, "I don't think so either. I'll have a word with someone and try and get you an immediate replacement for your passport. I'll leave messages at your lodgings but please feel free to phone my secretary as necessary." He wrote down her direct number. My friend's M.D. had never been given that.

I then read the fax. It was sensitive. The hot-shots had decided to go into business for themselves, only about twenty to thirty in all but all ex spies. They were specialists in destabilising regimes and imposing ones friendly to their masters. These were the hard men of the intelligence services who had been put out of work by the end of the Cold War These were bad bad people and I had been very lucky to survive. Did that make me a hero?

Pat's girlfriend's ex boyfriend was one of a number of psychopaths who had been used as disposable hit-men in the good old days. The word had it they were still disposable hit-men. It looked like we'd be disposing of one soon. I didn't tell the Senior Partner of my thoughts.

If any of these people were to have an accident or vanish no-one would ask too many questions. The Senior Partner agreed with this sentiment but stated that I ought to beware of the consequences in the U.K.. The audience was at an end, I left.

My new friend looked at me again in awe, You've spent more than ten minutes with the Senior Partner and that's unheard of, my friends won't ever believe this, and you're not even wearing a suit!"

I went to the range and put another hundred rounds into a target. This was practice but I needed a jungle lane and a carbine, not a formal range and pistol. I wasn't going to get a jungle lane, so this would have to do. I was firing with either hand and both hands; rapid and deliberate fire. The range officer was looking at me in a very strange manner. He was no fool and must have realised that I was preparing for something, especially since I had come to the range twice in two days instead of the usual once a month.

It was time to see Pat and tell him the bad news. He was in his room at the digs. He was not surprised when I told him about the hot-shots and the disposable hit-men. His comments were along the same lines as my earlier thoughts.

I made him talk to me about where his girlfriend was staying. It was his old flat. I made him draw plans of it. I made him tell me as much as he could of the bad guys and their methods, again, and again, and again.

A letter was dropped through the letter box, it was for Pat. It was two sets of keys and two maps of the location of the lock-up. He wanted to go and look. I forbade it, he had been out the previous night and it would be out of character to go out again that night, besides he needed his sleep.

I watched a bit of T.V. and went to bed early. I got up early too; not as early as Pat, but I surprised the landlady. I was going to recce the flat. I went into a charity shop and bought some intentionally ill fitting clothes. Dull inconspicuous and worn. Something that someone who was trying not to be down and out would wear. The clothes of someone who is ignored because he doesn't exist. I also bought a nerd's jacket and bobble hat. I went back to the digs and changed into my scruffy clothing.

I left by the back door and took a bus and then a tube to Paddington.

I managed to get slightly dirty and scruffy on the way. I walked around the area of the lock-up but only once past it. By the time I had finished I knew how to get there from any direction, day or night. I then took the bus to the neighbourhood around Pat's flat. More carefully this time, I played the same game. I needed to work out all the options for our arrival and getaway. It would be a getaway, and a nasty one at that.

What could go wrong? I had to think of all the what ifs? Remember, proper planning and preparation prevents piss poor performance.

I entered the digs through the back entrance, put my scruffy gear away, showered and changed. I went down to supper, which was early as usual.

I told Pat what I had done that day. He wanted to get on with things. He told me that he had received another note which discussed the arrangements for getting into Spain. He had to get to Belgium and meet a trucker on any Thursday at eight o?lock in the evening at a particular café in The Hague. They would be passed on until they reached the Costa Blanca. "All you've got to do is to work out how we get to us to Belgium."

I paid an extra two weeks rent to my landlady. This was a good place to stay and I didn't want to think about minor administrative matters. I reckoned that I would have got Pat out within two weeks. I watched the news; there was an item about poor quality drugs on the streets, addicts were being hospitalised and the police were giving the usual warnings. I spent the rest of that evening watching T.V..

The next day, I got up early. I then went into the local hospital and made a phone call to both the Manchester and York consultancies. I needed the background noise of the hospital. Thanks but no thanks to Manchester. In the case of

York, I told them that I had come down with some mysterious tropical disease; the doctors didn't think that I would recover for at least a month, and would they keep my offer open? I still had a job in the future.

If and when it was time to go, I wanted to be ready.

On the way back to the digs, I bought two wigs which I saw in a market. They were for women but I reckoned that a pair of scissors would soon solve that. I got back changed into a pair of jeans, my nerd jacket and bobble hat and went to the lock-up.

The lock-up was big and Bookie had done everything that he had promised. The only difference was that there was no C-4, he'd given me Semtex instead and the old stuff, so it wasn't traceable.

I returned to the digs and changed into my scruffy gear, except that I also put on one of the wigs. I went and watched Pat's flat. I hung around for the rest of the day and well into the night. The girlfriend left twice in the day and there were two goons with her. At night, a car came to fetch her, it was nine o'clock. They had left the place empty without a guard. They'd left the kitchen window open and it was an easy step from the fire escape.

I looked around inside. A nice normal flat. Only one bedroom was being used, so her guards must be doing shifts. That was no good. I looked at her clothes, she was going to need some stuff when she left. I stole a couple of sets of underwear, a pair of jeans, blouse, jacket and a pair of sensible shoes. I found a plastic bag. Folded her stuff into it and left. I hoped that she wouldn't notice, and if she did, she wouldn't say anything. She returned at three in the morning. It was a long trip back to the digs, even using the night bus.

There was a note for me when I got back, it was from Bookie. The ex boyfriend was now into pushing drugs. He was the cause of the bad drugs that were on the news. Nice people. The note also said where they were working from. I went to bed.

I missed breakfast, but I managed to slip out the back in my scruff gear. I went and did a recce at the ex boyfriend's H.Q.. It was a really grotty dive near Soho. Lots of strip joints nearby. In fact, his place was a strip joint cum club at the very bottom of the market. I wouldn't be out of place. I went in. There were a number of American hard men and even some hard women, coming and going from a door which led upstairs. He was not being very subtle. His goons looked the type who would be armed to the teeth. I could see why London's underworld were worried, he had an army and was about to start a war.

Well, Pat and I were an Army and we could also start a war. I went round the back and saw the kitchen exit. A steel door which appeared rusted shut - a great fire hazard. Well, I'll see to that! There were some disused sheds nearby, They were pad locked. I pulled hard on one and the screws pulled straight out of the wood; I couldn't believe my luck. It was half full of junk and obviously hadn't been used in ages, but there was enough room for the two bikes.

I went back to the B & B and got washed and changed into normal clothing. There was a phone call for me. Could I come urgently to visit the Senior Partner. I wore a suit this time. I thought that I would be less conspicuous. I think that it was appreciated.

"Tiffany's been abducted! They have killed or wounded all eight of her body guards. Her father receives a phone call every twelve hours from her. He has to stop his investigations. The Senior Partner was quite beside himself, "Didn't you know that I'm her Godfather? What the hell am I going to do?"

"Shut up and listen!" My friend of the last visit wouldn't have believed it, it worked. "Can you make covert contact with Tiffany's father?" He nodded, good. "I want him to do everything that he's told and to stop using the security company." He nodded again. "Can you make arrangements independently in the States?" He nodded yet again.

"Good. I need a small, very professional operation with no contacts to the C.I.A., F.B.I., N.S.A. etc., etc. to bug the phones and trace where the calls were coming from." He nodded. He was getting to be like one of those animals on the back windows of a car. I gave him a kit list which I would require when I got to the States; his eyes almost burst out of his head.

"Yes, it can be arranged." He was clearly out of his depth. "How are you going to get to the States without a Passport? Why aren't you leaving immediately?" He whined. He really was out of his depth.

"I've got to do some things here first, before I leave." I explained, "If what I do here works, it may make life in the States a lot easier, and you don't want to know what I'm up to. I need a contact number where I could reach you anytime." He wanted to give me several numbers. "Get a mobile phone and leave the number at the digs. Do it now."

He did his nodding dog impersonation again, in agreement. I left.

I phoned Bookie on that special number. "I need information. I need to know when our friends are going to do a big drug deal, but it has to be at his club, if possible."

"I get back to you soonest." was his reply, and he rang off.

I took a train to Folkestone. I had planned to do this so I had taken the trouble of taking my passport and suitcase with a suit and enough other stuff for about two weeks with me. In Folkestone, I opened an account in my Irish name. I said that

I would collect the cards and cheque book a few days later. I rented a room for a month and left the luggage. I paid cash so that there was no need for credentials. I returned to London. I missed supper, much to the landlady's annoyance.

Pat didn't need to know the bad news. I did warn him that we would soon get his girlfriend out but that it would be a very dirty job. He liked the idea. I told him about the club.

Pat and I went out for a drink. I told him, "I'm going to test the bikes. Tomorrow night we're going to put the bikes into the sheds, if they work O.K.."

"I was right, I knew you'd come up with a plan!" He grinned all the way back.

Next morning, I dressed in my nerd's gear. I bought a couple cheap packs that I could easily convert into saddlebags and went to the lock-up. All the gear worked. I filled the saddlebags with spare fuel. We were ready to deliver that night. I phoned the landlady to tell her that I would be missing supper, and did I have any messages? "Just a strange telephone number."

I went to another charity shop and bought scruff gear which would fit Pat and then I went to the cinema. Afterwards I had supper at a small Italian restaurant. Real food at last, which wasn't boiled to bits. I met Pat at the lock-up, carrying my scruff clothing, as arranged. Thankfully he had changed out of his postman's uniform. I put his scruff gear along with mine in the van.

It was very busy around the club and nobody noticed us putting the bikes in the shed. We covered them in old tarpaulins and I was sure that they wouldn't be noticed. We returned the van to the lock-up and got back to our digs somewhat late.

I had spent a week in the U.K. and I was ready not only to leave but to cause mayhem in the process. I tried the Senior

Partner's new number, it worked but he wouldn't know anything until that night. He told me that he liked his new toy and said goodbye.

I phoned Bookie the next day and he told me, "A deal's going down tomorrow night at half past ten at the club. Will you be ready?"

"I'm as ready as I am ever going to be."

"That's good. You know that despite you being an officer, you'd have made a great N.C.O.." I took that as a great compliment. I rang off.

I met Pat at the pub at lunchtime and told him, "It's on for tomorrow night."

"Thank God. I was afraid that she'll think that I've forgotten her."

I continued, "Pack for the trip, one small bag for you and another for some stuff that I nicked from her flat." He looked at me in awe.

"I've got to give in my notice so that the Post Office won't start looking for me." I thought that it was a bit late, but it would have to do.

We met back to the digs, Pat to pack and for me to check that everything was ready. We went out to dinner in anticipation of the next day. There would be no time for congratulations after the raid.

After we got back to the digs, I had time to think. Not only was I going to kill people, I was going to do it in cold blood. A lot of people in cold blood. But these people were murdering addicts by giving them bad stuff and they had tried to kill me, and were probably still trying to kill me, if they found me. Executing these killers may be the only way that I would survive my return to Britain.

CHAPTER 15

The Raid & Getaway

I phoned the Senior Partner first thing in the morning. "I'm happy to say that I've arranged all your requirements for the States although the tracing had not yet produced results."

"Good. Book me on tomorrow evening's flight from Paris to the States, business class, I commanded. I was being Napoleon again. "As Tiffany's father lives in Wilmington, it doesn't matter whether it's Washington or New York,. You'll have to arrange discrete accommodation and I'll need to be met at the airport. I gave him my Irish name and passport details; he didn't sound surprised. I'll also need a business visa for the States."

"It will all be arranged." he said and rung off.

I cleared all my stuff out of the digs and told the landlady that I had to go up north. I took all my stuff up to my flat, repacked it with my other clothes and put cases back with the two trunks. Nobody had checked the flat, I was sure, but it wouldn't matter if the goons came back. I went to an estate agent and arranged for them to pack everything up and store it and to sell the place. I'd tell them where to send all my stuff. I also told them that I'd suddenly got a good job up north but didn't yet have a contact number as I was going to one of a number of sites. I paid for the packing and the first three month's storage. I gave them a standing order for subsequent storage and they had my bank account details to deposit the money from the sale. I signed a letter of authorisation, and left.

I left wearing my nerd's gear. I was ready. I had four hours to kill before I met Pat at the lock-up so I had something to eat and went to see a movie.

We met as arranged. Pat put his travelling luggage in the van. We drove out and parked the van in a suitable place about a mile away from the club. We put the scuff clothing over our getaway clothing and hid our weaponry under our coats. I picked up the explosives and we started walking. It was eight o'clock.

We hung around for about half an hour, then we checked the bikes. We could see that they hadn't been visited, then I got to work. I rigged up explosives to blow the kitchen door when I pressed the transmitter. I put small charges in buckets at the back, just to cause bangs and we were ready. I managed to put a charge against the wall of the bouncer's booth. I had to be careful only to cause injury to the bad guys, not the patrons. We paid and went inside. We bought some of the watered down beer and started to sip it just like the other patrons.

I went to the loo and deposited another small charge over the loo which was unusable and returned. We waited. We had to endure a number of very poor quality acts. They were remarkably similar. However, they were met with great enthusiasm by the crowd, so we joined in. We'd made sure that we were far enough back not to be called upon to participate. Everybody was having a good time except the strippers, waitresses, bouncers and us. We ordered two more pretend beers; "You the last of the big spenders?" We had to keep sipping or we would have been thrown out.

We were just starting to watch the acts for the second time, when the girlfriend arrived. Pat started to get up and I had to restrain him. Twenty minutes later, a group of three heavies and a somewhat more refined gent walked straight through and went upstairs. The refined gentleman carried a large briefcase. I hoped that he expected to fill it. I didn't know if he was buying or selling; it didn't matter, there would be a lot of cash in the room.

I needed everyone to settle down before we moved. One of the ex boyfriend's goons and one of the heavies stood at the bottom of the stairs inside the door. We could see this as a waitress went up. We waited, the waitress came down, I gave it two minutes then we moved. Well, we moved when there were no goons around. The bouncers were walking in and out the room. We put on rubber gloves.

Another waitress started to go towards the door leading upstairs with a tray of drinks. We followed. I now had the .22 in my hand. The waitress had on a very skimpy number, and as the door was closing, I could see that the two guards were trying to look up her skirt, as she walked up the stairs. We slipped in just as they were turning back. We were the last thing that they saw. I shot each of them in the eye. Only the sound of the hammer falling, the slide moving and a sort of phut. No-one noticed. We sat them down in a manner to make them look like they resting on the stairs and then went up.

We could guess which was the office. We glimpsed the waitress entering the end door. There were two doors on each side. On the left, the first was open and led into a kitchenette. There were a goon and goonette, making eyes at each other. Both in the Rambo black sleeveless T-shirt. Six rounds later they were down, and still nobody noticed. I changed magazines and reloaded the used one.

The office door opened again, we closed the kitchen door and each pocketed a goon's handgun. Pat waved to me when the coast was clear. We listened for the scream when the waitress noticed that the guards downstairs had been shot. Nothing; maybe she was dozy or she took one look and decided to get out. I don't know but it worked to our advantage. We could hear a lot of raucous laughter in the room across the passage so I took out my remaining Semtex and put it on and around the door with radio receivers. Pat nodded, he understood.

The next door on the left was a lavatory, empty. The opposite door was locked, it was therefore not important. We'd check if there was time.

We opened the office door. On either side of a table sat the two principals, each with two goons behind them. The gent was testing white powder, the ex boyfriend was counting dollar bills, lots of dollar bills. Pat raised the Ingrams. Three of the goons went for guns. I fired two rounds into each of them. One stopped, the other two struggled, so I walked up and put another two rounds into those two; they stopped moving. I put my finger to my lips; the others kept quiet. I changed mags again, and again reloaded the old one.

Pat waved them all to one side and told them to sit on the couch. They did. I took a quick look at the money. Piles of one hundred dollar bills, and a few piles of Stirling. I quickly halved the pile. I wanted them to think that this was just a robbery. I put my half down my shirt. I pointed my .22 at the three of them and Pat disposed of his half. I told the ex boyfriend to call in Pat's girlfriend. The gent tried to push himself out of the chair. He got two rounds in the head and neck for his trouble. He had been going for a gun in an ankle holster. I pushed him back against the couch. Holding the .22 near the remaining heavy's head I searched him and removed his gun. The gent had only the one.

That left one heavy and the ex boyfriend.

I asked Pat, "Would you care to search lover boy?"

"It's my pleasure," so he hit him. Lover boy was armed with a gold plated Colt .45. He was asked again if he would care to call in Pat's girlfriend. He agreed this time and called her. I waited by the door. She came in accompanied by a goonette. The goonette succumbed to three rounds of .22 in the back of the head. No-one said a thing and then Pat's girlfriend started to recognise Pat; so did the ex boyfriend.

She told us, "There's another seven in the room along the passage." then pointing, "What you're going to do that bastard?"

Pat asked quietly, "What you would like us to do with him?"

"Shoot off his balls!" So he did!

He then shot the remaining heavy in the chest and I pressed the transmitter. All hell let loose. There were explosions everywhere. Then there was screaming from downstairs.

I swapped the .22 for the shotgun. I ran to the room along the passage and I threw in the baked bean grenade, which I had kept, and burst in after it went off. I shot three of the goons with the shotgun. Pat burst in immediately behind me, emptying the magazine of his Ingrams in bursts at anyone or anything that moved. There were no survivors. I reloaded the shotgun and he changed magazines. He then fetched his girlfriend and the three of us went down the stairs, me first and Pat last.

The remaining goons were running towards the stairs when we reached the bottom of them. The shotgun miraculously became empty again. So did the dance floor. I reloaded and we both advanced to clear up any opposition. It had gone. We went through to the kitchen. The staff were hiding huddled in a corner, we ignored them and ran outside through what was left of the steel door. As we ran out on our way, the staff ran out the other way, straight into the surviving goons who had decided to return.

We wrenched open the hut door and in turn, started and got out the bikes. While Pat was getting his girlfriend on the back; there was some difficulty due to the tight dress that she was wearing, I put two rounds from the shotgun into the kitchen entrance, reloaded and then fired another four.

We could hear sirens. We were in the middle of London Town and had started, and finished a war. It was time to go. It had taken us less than six minutes from the moment when we had reached the stairs to leaving the building, less than two minutes from the time that I had pressed the transmitter.

We had recce'd a couple of routes and discussed alternatives. The advantage of motor bikes is that they can go down narrow alleys and up and down steps. We were not exactly dressed for the occasion so we kept off the main drag. We also thought it would be very stupid to get run over by fast cars with blue flashing lights coming the other way. Pat led the way, and I kept an eye on the rear. We were free and clear.

We arrived at the van. It was still in the shadows. We lifted Pat's bike into the back, and took off the scruff gear. He would dump the bike in the country in Hertfordshire, and then dispose of all their clothing. They would then go on to Northampton where they would leave the van and take a coach to Felixstowe and the boat to Ostend. They would stay in The Hague, or nearby until they could get their lift to Spain. Quick goodbyes, and then they were off. I took all the weapons and my scruff clothing and stuffed them in the saddle bags; it was my responsibility to get rid of the guns. I put on the helmet which I had taken out of the van and I was back to being a nerd on a dirt bike.

I circled around to the west and then south. I was tempted to look at the chaos which we had caused but that could have led to problems. I stopped for a few minutes to refill the tank, soon after crossing into Kent. Later on, I noticed a wooded area and dumped the guns into a stream running through it.

I took my time and even stopped at an all night truck stop for a lousy cup of coffee and a worse toasted sandwich. I reached one of the last stops on the train before Folkestone at about five thirty. I parked the bike some distance away and removed the number plates, but left the keys and helmet. I hoped that it would get stolen.

I waited for the milk train and got into Folkestone at about six. By twenty past, I was in my rented room. I rolled up my nerd's and scruff gear and put it into a plastic bag ready for disposal. I counted my ill gotten gains. I had just under quarter of a million dollars and a few thousand pounds. I kept ten thousand dollars and put the remaining dollars in a plastic bag. I put the pounds in another.

I set the alarm on the watch which I had stolen from Y'all's goon and got a couple of hours sleep. The communal bathroom was grotty but by the time that I had finished, I looked respectable in my semi casuals and wiped the place for prints. I didn't think that it was necessary but they do it in the movies. I locked up and left, dumping my old clothing into a dustbin on my way to the bank.

I deposited the pounds in the bank account which was in my own name and the dollars in an offshore dollar account in my new Irish name. I also put one thousand dollars into my Stirling account in the Irish name. They would link the two accounts and "Wasn't it wonderful what you could do; fancy selling building sand to the Arabs?" They gave me my check book and cards. I left.

I walked down to the road and got a minicab to the hovercraft terminal. By midday, I was in France and five hours later, I was at the Charles de Gaul airport reception in Paris to collect my plane ticket. I was on the flight three hours later.

Red-eyes are always bad flights and I was jet lagged. The service was O.K. but I wasn't really in the mood. I was met by a real boffin type who introduced himself as Henny and who wouldn't stop talking. We were going to the office.

They were a very recent company. They were all computer geeks who were into computer fraud and anti-hacking. Someone else had supplied the weapons and they thought that I was some sort of James Bond. "We've tracked down the source of the calls to the State of Louisiana. You're on the morning flight to New Orleans and then onto Baton Rouge. You'll have all the necessary kit supplied in Baton Rouge. Henny's the lucky one who's going with you. The rest of us need to stay to manage the equipment."

I phoned the Senior Partner on his new cell phone. "I've been met and all appears to be under control."

"I'm impressed with the impact that you had on our friends. The media is running the story as if it was a gas explosion. How did you do it?"

My usual reply, "Did what? You don't want to know."

"I had dinner with a chap from the Home Office, an old school chum. He told me that they hadn't a clue as to what was going on. Oh, my chum will look into your passport. Where are you officially?"

I suggested, "Try something like camping somewhere in the Lake District or Scotland, maybe Wales or walking Hadrian's Wall. Be vague and generally unknowledgable, the sort of thing that happens when someone is pissed off, out of their depth, and otherwise generally depressed."

"Excellent idea."

I continued, "I'm moving. You'll get more details through the secure link. Contact your chum again, and suggest to him that it may be a drugs war between two American organisations, and that fit young Americans of both sexes who have Rambo T-shirts should be watched, especially if they have anything to do with the club which had blown up.

He said, "I'll get on with it. I hope Tiffany will be all right." and rang off.

I hoped so too, but I really didn't think that she stood much of a chance.

And then I had a nasty thought. They say "Y'all" in Louisiana as well as Texas, and as far as the States were concerned, it wasn't that far relatively speaking.

We landed at New Orleans. Henny had hired a 4 x 4, he thought it was cool, I thought that it was sensible. We stopped off on the way to get more suitable clothing, as I only had respectable clothing and Henny had dudegear. We drove to a type of chalet hotel near Baton Rouge, which the geeks had arranged. It was a sort of holiday place for campers who couldn't be bothered to camp. It had all the facilities and was fairly remote and quiet, in as much as these places can be remote and quiet. A large suitcase was in reception waiting for us. It contained the kit.

I looked at the kit at leisure. I was getting expert in this; I had a Browning, a six shot snubby, and another silenced .22. There was a G.P.S., a cell phone and a laptop computer with a map package. The laptop could be linked to the G.P.S. allowing us to see our actual location on the map. Clever stuff.

I asked him, "Can get me more weaponry, and if so, what? What do you carry? Can you find me a range around here?"

Henny had become very business like, "Yes. What's your shopping list? None, I don't know how to shoot. Give me five minutes" He came back literally five minutes later. "I want your shopping list in writing and I've found a secluded spot that we can legally use as a range.

He thought that the bad guys were using a computer system but using it from a cell phone, they may have identified part of the simcard code. I didn't understand a bloody thing that he said, but after a time I understood the words of a single syllable.

I got the general idea. He thought that it may have coming from the Bayous. Now, that made real sense. You're based in the middle of a swamp. Easy to defend and you get in a boat and change you position every time you send a message. Your base could even be that boat.

I was still concerned about Texas but you don't shit on your own doorstep, so you do the naughties elsewhere. If you're based in Texas, the Bayous were as good as anywhere. If we were going to play in the Bayous, I wanted the best odds that I could get. Actually I wanted the very best odds that I could get. I wrote down my wish list: a sniper's rifle, a very large capacity short range weapon like a P.P.Sh-41, a pair of snubbies and a semi auto Mini-Uzi with lots of magazines for Henny, and a fast boat with a shallow draft powered by water jets.

I was getting a lot of expensive kit, and I wasn't paying for a single item, it was great.

I heard a buzzing sound, and looked up. I could see a microlite, or ultralite as they call them in the States. I always wanted to learn how to fly but had never got round to it. I then saw another, and realised that there must be a strip nearby. Then I saw something that really caught my attention; a parachute with a small engine on the pilot's the back. I had jumped a couple of times when I was younger, when I had had aspirations of being Rambo, and I realised that it wouldn't take many hours to learn how to fly one of these. It would take up little space and be an instant recce aircraft or means of infiltration.

It would take at least twenty four hours to get the extra kit, so I was going flying the next day. I got into the 4 x 4 and drove to the airstrip. I could start the next day. I used some of my wad of stolen cash to pay for the course.

CHAPTER 16

Airborne & Waterborne

I got up really early and went down to the strip. I had to learn a whole new technique. This was a steerable chute. I then had to learn how to be lifted off the ground by cable, just like a glider. It was fun! I couldn't believe it, I was good. I mean really good. By lunchtime I'd got the hang of it and was ready to move to the powered chute.

By the end of the afternoon, I was doing short take-offs. By the end of the next day I'd be able to fly one of these. I got back to Henny. He thought that I was mad. He'd made progress. The weapons would be delivered the next day. There was one problem the supplier couldn't get a P.P.Sh-41. Would an A.M. 180 do? I wondered what one of those was. He told me that it was an SMG in .22 with a 177 round magazine. He showed me a picture and the specs.

The internet is a wonderful thing. This A.M. 180 was just what the doctor ordered. If he confirmed at once, it would be supplied with the other weapons; I told him to go ahead, I then told him to suspend the order for the Uzi; he looked really downhearted, and to get two A.M.180's and a total of at least ten magazines; he cheered up considerably.

He had already arranged for the boat and it would be ready from the day after. He didn't know what time the weapons delivery would take place. I suggested that he could drop me off at the air strip, and I would get a lift or taxi back.

We ate supper at a local diner. The food was greasy but the people were nice and we had a good time. We got back fairly early because of the early start the next day.

We started early the next day. I got my wings by the end of the afternoon and straightaway bought a powered chute, and tested it. I nearly killed myself I was so overconfident. This taught me a real lesson and I became a better pilot because of it. I didn't bother with the lift or taxi, I just flew it back to the chalet. Henny was really impressed, but he still thought that I was mad.

The weapons were all there. I'd been given an FN FAL as the sniper's rifle. I wasn't expecting one of those, but you don't get any better. I really wanted to test the gear.

Henny told me that we could test the weapons at a place that we could visit on the way to see the boat. It would only be a half hour out of our way. We were almost ready. We went back to the diner and then onto a local bar. Everybody was wearing cowboy hats and singing in old French. It was great fun, but Tiffany's plight was always at the back of my mind. I went outside and phoned the Senior Partner.

He informed me that the two daily calls were continuing and that from the questions that Tiffany was allowed to answer, she was genuinely alive. Special Branch had pulled in some people and it looked like there would be some convictions. The drug squad had also done similar. Altogether about twelve people had been arrested. The black T-shirt thing had worked. This time I rung off. I wondered about my passport.

Henny was starting to get drunk and was eyeing one of the barmaids; I thought that this could lead to a fight as her boyfriend was sitting at the bar, so I made him get up and we left. They waved to say thanks, which I thought was nice. I put

Henny to bed, he was worse than I had thought and I started to clean the shipment of weapons. I put the two holsters on my belt and started to wear the two handguns. I was starting to get into the mood again.

I woke up at dawn and had a shower before making breakfast with lots of coffee and orange juice. Henny needed it, but by eight o'clock we were leaving. I wanted to test the weapons and see the boat.

That FN FAL was a joy. I had to use a clip-on bi-pod but I was hitting head sized objects at six hundred meters, rapid, which is brilliant for me. The A.M. 180 was an absolute wonder. I almost cut an old car in half with a single magazine, and it was totally controllable in fully auto mode.

Henny was good with the A.M. 180, but anybody would be good with one of those, but he was an absolute natural with the FN FAL, I was quite jealous. Unfortunately, he was pretty useless with any of the hand guns; he couldn't even hit the target at five meters with the Browning, and only managed to get three out of five on the same target with a revolver. I told him not to use a handgun until he could see the whites of the enemy's eyes. Still, to use a handgun properly takes a lot of practice, and we could only spare a couple of hours on his revolver technique.

We went on to see the boat. There had been a cock-up. It was already hired out to someone else. The only thing he could do was to let us have a normal speed boat, or if we must have a boat with water jets, he knew of a yard that sometimes hired out an old mark II inshore patrol boat from the Viet Nam days. It was a bit bigger than we had asked for, but that's all he could do.

I took a look at her. She was a bit scruffy outside but clean down below. She was converted to make her more of a week-end boat, and she was a bit long in the tooth but she could still do twenty four knots. Henny said "no," I said "yes." She was everything that I could wish for. She had a shallow draft, fast, powered by water jets and armoured. We could live on board and search for Tiffany.

We paid for two weeks hire with an option for longer and moved straight on board. It took a little time to get the weapons aboard without being noticed and Henny went back to get some of our clothes, his electronic gear and my power chute. By half past four, we were ready to leave. The great thing about the G.P.S. is that it also works with computerised charts. A lot of the Bayous are charted so we had some sort of idea what to expect.

We moved into the Bayous. He was right about the cell phone. He had developed some sort of gizmo which identified the cell phone and the geeks were able to tell which relay station was being used. We spent the night at a very pleasant landing.

We knew that the calls occurred at fairly regular times, so we planned around it. I found this worrying. Why would they allow two calls a day unless they were planning something critical and needed to keep anybody but especially daddy from nosing around.

They were ex spooks. They were a small (?) group from all (?) over the world. They were probably predominately based in the U.S.. With modern communications, did they need to run it from the U.S.? The top boys didn't need to be in the U.S., they just needed to have a quiet life and control the operation. Still, I would know nothing until I got Tiffany safe and found someone senior on whom I could use a set of pliers.

We were ready for the transmission the next morning. We got our fix. We went to the relay station, there was nothing. We had the same problem that evening.

The two calls the next day confirmed that they were moving around. I hired a light plane and pilot and was in the air waiting for a transmission. The geeks got a fix, but it was near a very public waterway. We tried again that evening, we were lucky!

There was a single suitable craft on that waterway. We watched it until it went into some thick cover. There were only four large houses in the area. It became too dark to continue so we landed. Henny and I went looking. By dawn we were more or less at the centre of the search area. We hid the boat overlooking the largest waterway and waited. We saw no movement, but we knew which direction they should be coming from.

That meant only one house. We moored alongside the island out of sight of the house. We were generally well hidden, even from the air. I went ashore with the A.M. I also had a pair of binos and a ghillie suit which I had included in my kit list.

Unless you have dogs or high technology on your side, it is extremely difficult to maintain the initiative when you are guarding something. This is why special forces are so often successful. It is almost impossible to keep everyone switched on. It's just another day for the guard. He doesn't know when the infiltration or the attack will start, or even if there will be one. For the infiltrator or attacker, this is a known moment of acute danger and so he is much more aware and ready for action.

I was scared shitless, but I crept forward until I had a good vantage point overlooking the grounds. I had to be careful. The top of the house covered most of the island, so there was a high probability of being seen unless I took considerable care. During daylight hours all they really needed was one person on each side of the house in a room on the top floor or attic. If he or she was careless I'd see him (or her). Gotcha! he moved the curtain. He appeared to be shooing something out the window. Thanks Ms. Bee, or whatever. He'd got a Heckler & Koch MP5 with all the trimmings, so this place wasn't Kosher. It had taken a week but I had found her.

I crawled back to the boat and briefed Henny. I wanted to know who owned the house. We didn't have a field telephone and I was afraid that radio or cell phone communications may be picked up by equipment that they may have. Henny informed his colleagues using a parabolic aerial direct to a satellite. I went back to watching. I didn't learn a hell of a lot more. They mostly stayed in the house and I counted four goons and a goonette. They'd all got the Rambo T-shirt. What was this, a uniform? One woman in a dress, not Tiffany, came out of the house. She walked around the house, having a smoke. I couldn't tell if she was checking the place or if she was just taking a break.

I went back to the boat. Bad news, it was standard procedure for them to inform the police if any situation broke, and the office manager had done that without being told, despite the fact that he had been informed to do nothing until I had O.K.'d it!

I told Henny, "Start up if any unusual activity occurs and be prepared to move the boat around the island as necessary. Even to be prepared to shoot up or ram their boat if you can see that Tiffany isn't on board." I switched my phone back on but turned off the ring tone with Henny's help. Paranoia, I guessed that the bad guys would find out so I had to do my hero bit and try and get in. Maybe I could get her out or hole up and wait for the fifth cavalry.

Henny said, "I should come with you to give covering fire with my A.M. or the FN FAL, if you need it. I'll be able to see what's happening and it'll take no time to get down the boat and get it started." This was not such a stupid idea. We retied the boat with quick release knots and set off.

I set him up in a good position, made him comfortable, and tried to find a way in. I took me a good hour to get to within twenty meters of the house, then I was stuck. I had twenty meters of lawn to cross. I had to wait until it got dark. They switched on the outside lights a dusk; thankfully they were designed for beauty and to allow people to walk around in the grounds at night. These lights caste shadows, so it was a case of moving from shadow to shadow.

I was able to do the Raffles bit. There was a creeper up one of the walls and even an open window. I went for it. I crept in. There was no-one on the first floor. There were voices coming from downstairs. They were expecting Tiffany back soon, I hadn't heard or seen her leave. I went back to my room and waited. The woman in the dress went out to meet them at the jetty and escorted her back. She was either the minder or the boss. Either way she would be formidable and probably very cunning.

Everyone came back inside and sat down. There were moans about food and whose turn it was to cook, and why didn't they have trained cooks on these sorts of operations, because they used to before they privatised. I crept into the attic. I expected to find sentries with night vision aids, but nothing.

I had now counted at least nine people, including the well dressed woman. That is not to say that they others weren't well dressed, but they had stripped their tops down to those bloody T-shirts.

There was a shout from downstairs. Now what? "We're blown! They know where we are and they're on their way!"

I phoned Henny, "The bad guys know so be ready to move. I'll see what I can do." I rung off.

I heard the whup, whup, whup of the rotors of what must have been UH-1, Hueys. Just loved it, a real covert operation! The bad guys would have no warning against this ultra quiet surprise attack, unless the cops, or was it the F.B.I. thought that a group of well trained operatives who had been trained to take on, and win, against ten times their number of M.V.D. troops were going to take one look at them and surrender. Fat chance.

I cocked the A.M. 180 and dashed down the stairs. The classy women had already grabbed Tiffany and was out of the door. The others were good, but the A.M. was better. I fired from the hip and hosed the room. The rate of fire is so high that, despite being a .22, the rounds cut through just about anything, or in this case anybody. By the time that the magazine was empty, they were all on their way to Hell.

By the time that I reached the door, I could see the two women, almost at the jetty. The classy women fired a couple of shots at me, but she'd have to have been bloody good or bloody lucky to have hit me. I couldn't return fire even with the A.M. in semi auto mode, because I had a high probability of hitting Tiffany. Anyway, I hadn't yet changed mags.

I heard two engines start almost simultaneously. Henny was quick off the mark. It took him about the same time to reach the jetty as it did me. He was even wearing our set of night vision goggles. I jumped aboard, and he gave the old girl welly. He followed the goons' cabin cruiser like a bat out of hell. Our patrol boat was an old lady, and badly abused; she did the best she could but even so, the cruiser started to slowly slip ahead.

I used the cell phone to contact the geeks and tell them the situation and watch for any signal from the cabin cruiser. I contacted daddy, and told him of the cock-up and of the fact that Tiffany was still alive. They must have needed her alive or she would have been dead. I got him to tell me about the ex spy organisation.

In short, it had become a private army with its own agenda. Knowledge of its existence had been lost but it still obtained funding because of the computerised system of funds allocation in existence. He had been part of a congressional special investigation into the intelligence community after the fall of the Berlin Wall and had discovered it, suggested that it be disbanded and stopped its funding. He probably knew more about it than any outsider. He gave me the co-ordinates of their old operations base and training centre in Texas. He said that he now thought that his security company may have had a few old members in it, which is how the goons knew where to find Tiffany.

I contacted the geeks. The woman had already contacted someone, they could tell when she had the cell phone on, and when she was using it. They could also tell which transmitter it was in contact with. More than that, it was impossible to say.

We could still see the cabin cruiser. There were only a couple of place where the goons would have sensibly left a car. I got all the gear packed and on deck ready to unload.

CHAPTER 17

By Road & by Air

We watched her smash the cabin cruiser straight up a launching ramp by the side of a marina, near our boatyard. I dropped the A.M. which I had been grasping and told Henny to go along side anything near the beached cruiser. I jumped ashore and watched them get into a large, or what was to me, large, saloon car. It was fairly dark but I couldn't tell the colour in the darkness.

She took another pot-shot at me and threw Tiffany into the car. She then had to drive through the security barrier. The guard was terrified but told me it was a dark blue Pontiac with a Texas number plate, KICK ASS I told him to call the cops and ran back to the old patrol boat. We went the extra three hundred meters to our own berth and tied up, then we started loading the kit into the 4 x 4.

We were five minutes behind but I reckoned that we knew which direction which she was taking. I couldn't understand why they still needed Tiffany, but I was grateful.

It took us a long time to get to Lafayette, and the road to Beaumont and Houston. The old command centre was about fifty kilometres, about thirty miles, further on past Houston. The geeks confirmed that she was heading west, about ten miles ahead of us. They'd informed the F.B.I. because kidnapping is a Federal crime. They hoped that something would happen.

I doubted that anything would. It's only in the movies that you get instant response by the cops. In reality it takes time to work out what is happening, put together a suitable team, issue orders, get the guys aboard a helicopter, lift off etc., etc.. Crossing a State line can also cause problems, as it means passing from one jurisdiction to another. However hard they tried, the geeks could not get a key figure in the chain of command to understand the connection between Tiffany, the raid on the island, the shooting on the dockside and our car chase. You always get one. Someone, probably the same idiot, wanted to arrest us, for speeding. Luckily, we didn't get caught.

I explained to Henny that we weren't going to stop at a police road block as we had too many weapons on board. He told me not to worry, they were all registered with the company, after all it was a security company, and I was a registered consultant with them. I put my foot down harder. There was no way that we could keep up with that Pontiac but we did the best we could. We passed over the Sabine River and therefore the State line and kept on going. From the geeks monitoring of our cell phone location and her cell phone location, we would probably arrive forty five minutes after the two women.

We were warned that the old command post was surrounded by a bloody great mine field, so it wasn't possible to drive off road to it. We needed to fuel up again at Beaumont. Henny took over. I had to keep putting my hand on his knee. No! Not for that, to push his foot harder on the accelerator; its a left hand drive vehicle. At least he had a sense of humour, and said, "I didn't know that you cared."

I started to prepare for the next round I was going to fly over the minefield using the power chute. I didn't tell Henny, he'd have stopped the car there and then! I was ready. I plugged in the G.P.S. and the laptop and fed in the co-ordinates of the command centre. I now knew how to get around the back of the complex. I sat back and forced myself to relax, only occasionally putting my hand on Henny's knee.

I then realised that I was a bit insane. I was going straight into the lion's den. With hindsight, I can see that being tortured in Zaire and then booby trapped in Surbiton had flipped my mind. The pressure of being some sort of superhero was pushing me over the edge. It was also at that point that I knew that I was in love with Tiffany. I must have fallen for her the moment she asked me to help her, in that awfully polite voice of her's. I knew that she couldn't cook and always used up all the hot water, but her manner, her intelligence and the fact that she could look good in a bin liner did a hell of a lot to overcome those minor disadvantages. Anyway, she wasn't an engineer or scientist, so she couldn't steal my job!

We arrived. It wasn't a building, it was a bloody great complex. I could see that it was a converted ranch. We had gone around the back and stopped on the brow of a hill about two kilometres away, or should I say a mile away since we were in the States. The whole place was surrounded by wire, in fact two rows of wire about a hundred meters apart. The minefield must have been in between.

I had been trained how to clear a minefield, but there just wasn't time to get in that way. The outer wire was within five hundred meters on one side of the building, but was a long way away on the other side. They had an airstrip within the wire. There were two aeroplanes on the apron, a twin executive jet and a twin prop cargo plane that looked a bit like a Hercules. The place was lit up like a Christmas tree and there was considerable activity. The light on the area was so intense that it was almost impossible to use the night goggles. Despite the activity, there were not many people around, about twenty that I could see.

I was going in. We drove about two miles back down the road and got out the power chute. I worked out a way to carry the A.M. under the harness, and started the engine. Henny was mumbling about madmen but told me, "I'll go down to the wire with the FN and offer you any support that I can." I took off.

Initially, I flew away from the complex and gained height. At about four thousand feet, I switched off the engine and started to glide towards the complex. There was a large patch of relative shadow and I headed for that. I managed to land without being observed and without hurting myself. I rolled up the chute and put it under a bush in the best secret agent fashion, and started to sneak towards the buildings.

There were no patrols, all the activity seemed to be centred around one building and the hanger adjacent to the airstrip. There was another building a little distance away from the activity, with all the lights on. I could see that people were still working, or at least it looked like they were working. In fact, it looked like a normal office block where people were working late.

I was approaching what I thought was the main complex building, when I heard a siren behind me and a Jeep with a machine gun mounted on top came screaming up the road from the direction of the main gate. I was not coming towards me; it was heading for a section of the main fence where Henny would be if he was near the main fence. Henny was near the main fence. They must have had geo-sensors!

The machine gun opened up and Henny returned fire with the FN FAL. Henny may have been a geek, but he sure as hell had guts. He'd taken cover and was slowly and deliberately returning fire, just as I had taught him. Four shots, three hits, which is remarkable for those conditions. Just about every other security guard in the complex, converged on the Jeep and they opened up as well, on Henny's position.

Henny had volunteered for this, and I was not about to waste his sacrifice. I kept on going.

My logic was that the main headquarters would be the place where they would hold Tiffany. I was wrong. When I arrived, the place was empty. The activity which I had seen with the goggles was people leaving the building. I ran out and heard screaming, the sound of breaking glass and a huge amount of machine gun fire. This time, it was coming from the office block. The security guards had stopped shooting at Henny and were looking at the office block in amazement.

There was a sudden silence. About half a dozen men dashed out of the building and ran towards the parked cargo plane. The jet was moving off down the runway, preparing to take off. The cargo plane started to follow it. The six men caught up with the plane and jumped in; the tail door closed.

I started running towards the hanger. It was empty but for a few crates and the Pontiac. I could block the runway with the Pontiac! But I couldn't, they'd taken the keys; and I still didn't know how to hotwire a car. There was nothing I could do; I heard the whine of all four engines, and then saw the jet take off immediately followed by the cargo plane.

I had screwed up! I should never of let Henny near the wire. I should have thought of the geo-sensors. It was also of little comfort to know that the organisation had probably planned to kill all the people in the office block anyway. But why? I couldn't tell.

I had to get out. The only way that I could think of was to get out the way that I had come in, but I wasn't about to do that with all the activity and shooting. I'd be noticed as soon as I started the motor.

Suddenly, the guards stopped firing. They roared into the hanger. I thought that I was finished and hid behind one of the few packing cases and prepared to sell my life dearly. There were a lot of comments about illegitimate people participating in sex and travel and further comments about how they must also participate in the same activities and then they roared back to the gatehouse. There was much shouting and running around, then everybody got into vehicles and they roared off into the night.

I phoned Henny, "Come and get me out of here." I walked into the office block. The place had been completely shot up. Then I realised that it was a computer centre. They needed to destroy the computer records but they had screwed up by not preparing to blow it up or wipe the files. There were many dead but still, a number of people survived. The survivors were in a daze. Most of the damage was on the first floor. The type of offices shot up suggested that it was the key figures and the mainframe room which had been the main targets. If you can't wipe the files and remove the key figures, destroy the computer and kill anybody who had access to the passwords etc..

Henny arrived, I phoned him using the cell and told him to come up to where I was. When he arrived, he told me that the goons had mostly shot up ancillary equipment and that it would be possible to access the data files. "Go for it."

I was curtly informed, "It's not a matter of walking away with a few floppy discs. I need to connect it by phone to the office computer and download that way. It'll be better to use a cell phone, and yours would be best as there was no connection between company, myself and its acquisition. The bad news is that I'll have to alter it and destroy it in the process."

"Get on with it then!"

While he was destroying my phone, I used his to phone the geeks' office and brief them, then Henny took over and briefed them some more, but relating to computer matters using computer speak. He then got on with the business in hand.

I used one of the land lines to call 911 and ask for an ambulance, or rather several ambulances. I just couldn't let the wounded die. I left Henny to continue monitoring the data file downloading and went to pack up and load the power chute. It didn't take me long. I really didn't want to leave any evidence if possible. The downloading was almost complete by the time that I got back. Both this computer and the geeks were very fast, or so I was told. At last, the downloading was complete, and Henny disconnected.

I suggested to Henny that we leave before the Feds arrived. There nothing we could do except check into one of the Holiday Inns in Houston, so we drove off.

We waited in our room for somebody to phone us on Henny'sphone. Somebody did, it was daddy. "Why can't I get through on your phone?"

I merely told him, "It's otherwise engaged and forget the number for a short while."

The geeks then phoned, "We're were already starting to break the security code. It's difficult but we've designed better, but by morning we'll be able to read the data base. We've found out by means which we won't reveal, that the planes have headed off in a south easterly direction. You'll need to get back to Washington. We took the first flight.

We left the Hotel separately; I took a taxi while Henny took the 4 x 4. We met again at the airport. Henny had taken our vehicle to a safe place as it contained all the weapons and kit.

If we were not going back to Houston, an associate company would arrange the return of the car to the hire company and the rest of the kit to Washington.

The geeks had had to transfer the data from their normal computer to a mainframe which they had somehow bodged up, well that's how I understood it. This thing was absolutely superb at number crunching. It had already worked out the method of encryption and the geeks were already looking at the data files when we arrived.

Tiffany's father was already there. I could feel that he was disappointed that I had not managed to free his daughter. I think that he understood that the cock-up at the island was not my fault, and that it was only partly my fault that things went wrong at the complex.

I did my Napoleon bit, "Speak to me people. I want to know two things. I want to know where on the planet they may be taking Tiffany, based on the flight direction and on any geographical data that may be in the data base. Secondly, I want to see their personnel files." They got someone onto the first request and daddy and I started to look at the personnel files. There was a lot more data available to him than during his investigation and he could't understand how the operation was still functioning after his recommendations had been made. He was on the phone most of the time while we looked at faces.

There seemed to be two groups of key figures. One group included mostly non Americans while the other group contained mostly Americans. My two hot-shots were in the non American group. The four types, two dead, whose photos I had seen on the hot-shots office wall were part of the American group. Deceased operatives were listed as such. A geek came in and down loaded another file which had been encrypted separately. We brought that lot up on the screen.

It appeared that this group were deep cover operatives who worked for the organisation. They worked within their own countries. There were even Americans. I found White Shirt in this group. I was flipping through the faces when Tiffany's dad swore and told us to go back one frame. He swore again. It was his ex son-in-law. He was labelled as dead, killed by an O.D. of some sort of drug during interrogation.

We looked at his record. He had been set up to spy on daddy through Tiffany. He couldn't stop the divorce. A memo stated that he had the only remaining copy of a series of numbers for numbered accounts in banks throughout the world and a whole stash of bearer bonds. The memo continued that the organisation thought that he had put it in some sort of joint account safe deposit, for safe keeping, but which was still being fought over by their two lawyers. That explained why they still needed Tiffany. It must be big, big, Big money. They had to wait for the financial settlement to be cleared before they could get access to the goodies. They had kept his death secret from the authorities. That would take at least another two weeks before they could access the safe deposit box.

There was a phone call for daddy. He was to go to the C.I.A. Building to be briefed, it was too sensitive to discuss over the phone. He left.

We continued to try to work out where the planes had gone. The geeks through a mixture of interpolation, and hacking into the N.S.A.'s, F.AA.'s, D.o.D.'s and State Department's computers worked out that they had flown to Caracas and then onto Belem, but they didn't continue on into Brazil. These boys were good!

I looked for a map, and found one. They may be going onto Argentina, well my nice new shiny Irish passport would get me in there. I booked a flight to Argentina, then I stopped and cancelled my booking. Sometimes I'm very stupid! I looked at the map again. I knew where they were going. With long range fuel tanks, it would be easy to cross the Atlantic. They were going back to Zaire. But why?

I went outside for some fresh air. I understood. The organisation had set up the kidnapping of Tiffany. They had used the four idiots to do this, but only Marie knew. Why did they need to ambush the Presidential vehicle? Why was I set up to replace an expert? A coincidence? Maybe the team of Americans had gone into business for themselves. Why share all that money with the others? Had the organisation found out and had the hot-shots been detailed to find Tiffany and kill the four Americans? But why Zaire?

I had to book a flight to Zaire, no! The hot-shots, the organisation seemed to have its interests in Eastern Zaire and I knew that this trip would be violent. No, I'll go to Uganda and slip across the border. I went back in and got to a phone. I booked the quickest set of flights to Uganda. I would take the last Concorde flight to Charles de Gaulle, Paris, and then take the flight to Entebbe. I'll get a bike and infiltrate in. It was a workable plan. Mustn't forget a nice big set of pliers for White Shirt!

Tiffany's father returned from his meeting. He had a lot to say. It was a United States responsibility to destroy the organisation, both within and outside the country. He said that the N.S.A. had just had pictures confirming that the two planes had crossed the Atlantic. The Intelligence community had now taken over and were starting to put an operation together. He was not to remain involved, but they would, of course, keep him fully informed, as a matter of courtesy.

He was astounded when I told him that I had already booked flights to get me to Entebbe, and that I intended to infiltrate into Zaire. I told him that I needed a satellite phone so that I could keep in contact, and that I needed to do a little shopping, a few items for camping in Zaire; dried food, a torch, a few clothes and a day bag etc.. I had left all my kit in Houston.

I wanted Tiffany's passport which must still be at the house. I also needed a pair of Tiffany's gym shoes; I wasn't going to see her walk long distances again in high heels!

We would meet for dinner before my flight.

CHAPTER 18

Return to the Concession & Back at the House

One has to drink champagne when one is travelling faster than the speed of sound. It's the only thing to do. Actually, its over rated; The reduced pressure affects ones sense of smell and taste and so the Champagne tasted very ordinary. After the first one, I stuck to orange juice. Otherwise the flight was quite pleasant.

There was the usual delay in transit at Charles de Gaulle, with nothing to do; and then the usual boarding procedures for the Air France flight to Uganda. Thankfully the hosties on this flight spoke better English than my schoolboy French and so the flight was O. K..

I was jet lagged when I got off the flight, and took a courtesy bus to the Speke Hotel in Kampala. When I was staying at the Sheraton, they told me that the Speke Hotel Restaurant served some of the best curry in Uganda, and I like curry. I checked in, and although desperate to go to bed, I went out and bought a Yamaha 175 DT. It was second hand but almost new. I was overcharged and paid cash from my stash of dollars. It was still registered in the previous owner's name, and it was up to me to re-register it.

I didn't bother. If I had problems or I had to leave it, I didn't need to leave evidence. It wouldn't bother the previous owner, he was an ex-pat and had completed his contract never to return; his wife couldn't handle Africa and being away from her family.

I bought some spare fuel cans and two stroke oil, and with the saddle bag kit which I had bought in Washington, I was ready to go. I went back to the hotel and went to bed.

I had dinner downstairs, and yes, the curry was excellent. What was even better, was that I saw no-one from the Embassy who I recognised, or who appeared to recognise me.

I settled my bill and left first thing in the morning. I took what I needed and left the unnecessary stuff in a suitcase which the Hotel kept for me. After all, I was going on a short trip and would be back in a few days. By early afternoon, I had reached the Lake View Hotel.

I had decided to stay there because I needed the number plates from the old bike. When I got into Zaire, I thought it wise to have Zairean plates.

The Hotel Staff looked surprised when I walked in, they were about to sell the bike for scrap. I told them to carry on and keep the cash but I wanted the plates as a keepsake. They were even more surprised with my Irish passport, but I said that my mother was Irish and I was entitled to dual nationality, and that was the Irish translation of my English name. They had met many Englishmen and Irishmen so this story did not seem to surprise them. I tipped them heavily in Dollars, and I hoped that this would keep their mouths shut whatever they really thought.

I left early the next day. By early afternoon, I had crossed the border and was back at the top of my conical hill. Paranoia rules! The weapons and all the other kit was fine. I was ready to go.

Although it was getting on, I decided that it was better to get away from the border, and left. I had travelled about fifty kilometres before I pulled off the road and set up a small camp. Mosquito repellent is wonderful stuff, it was the first night out in Zaire that I hadn't been bitten. I left soon after dawn, and this time, I did not get lost. I arrived at the concession soon after midday.

I set up a basha in the same place, and found both the food and my little dam. I was grateful for the remaining fuel. There was enough in total to get me to M'eni or back over the border. I started to examine the village. I was looking for the white Toyota. It wasn't there.

I phoned daddy on the satellite phone to keep him up to date. He had been worried because I had been out of contact so long. He told me that satellites had picked up the two planes in Kisangani. Now, why didn't this surprise me?

I suppose that I could have set off again that day, but I wanted to see if the hot-shots were at the mine and, besides my backside was numb and I was tired. I waited but no hot-shots and no plane. I wondered if I could get into their cottage but realised that I would have to break in, and I didn't want them to know that anybody was interested in them. I prepared supper but ate it cold at about eight o'clock. There was nothing else I could do so I went to sleep.

It was a very early start again in the morning. I was going to the cottage, but I was going to use the old disused plant road. It was quicker returning because I only had myself to worry about. I got to the old plant at about midday and it took me less that an hour to get near the cottage and house. I decided to become paranoid again. I drove the last couple of kilometres at low revs and stopped well short of the cottage track. I had a small pair of bino's so I didn't even take the P-14. I sneaky beakied towards the cottage via Jean's grave.

The grave had not been filled in and he was just white bones, and not many of them. This did not bode well. I knew that Fred wanted the grave filled in as soon as possible. I continued up to the cottage. It was empty. It seemed just as I had left it. Maybe, they didn't want to remember, or more likely they had decided to return to Belgium, but what about Fred? He would remain in Zaire. I hoped that it was a case of being on holiday but I was worried. Very worried.

These were nice gentle people who were no match for the organisation. The organisation wouldn't, and indeed hadn't, thought twice about squashing them like bugs. I sneaky beakied towards the house. The white Toyota double cab was there. Why hadn't they filled in Jean's grave? I could see lots of shit ahead.

I got near enough to use the binos usefully, and waited. Alphonse came out of the kitchen and went to the herb garden. He picked some herbs and returned. I could see Fred wandering around near one of the sheds. That was it. Despite the appearance of normality, something seemed wrong. I waited. Then I heard a woman's voice scream something in French. Marie? She hadn't been on the computer but there was nothing to say that she wasn't still being used.

I slipped around to where Fred was working. He was first shocked, then surprised and then delighted to see me. He almost shouted my name then he checked himself. "We got back and found the two hot-shots and Marie waiting for us. No-one had bothered about Jean, our cover story satisfied them for a couple of days. Then suddenly the hot-shots knew everything."

This appeared to be about the time that Tiffany had been kidnapped. The hot-shots came and went, but Marie remained, making them wait on her, hand and foot. The hot-shots had returned three days earlier leaving Tiffany and three goons and another woman at the house before leaving again. The woman seemed to be in charge. The woman on the island? That would figure.

What was I going to do? It was five to one. I asked Fred to tell me about supper arrangements. "Alphonse, Albert and I eat in the Kitchen while the others eat on the dining room. The big problem is that the woman always makes one of the goons stay on watch. He eats later. I think that the hot-shots have gone to the mine. That was possible but I hadn't seen them. Maybe they've been doing other business. Certainly the concession would be a great place to hide the personnel remaining in the organisation until they could find somewhere more suitable.

"Alphonse is making soup for tonight. I can cause a diversion by spilling it on Marie or the other woman. They always serve the food. You can come in and shoot the place up after you've killed the guard. They eat late so it'll be dark, and it'll be easy to sneak up on him." Bloody hell, he had real faith in me! I couldn't think of anything better, so we agreed on it.

I asked Fred, "Get me one of those bloody great kitchen knives that Alphonse likes, but sharpen the bloody thing first." I would have preferred a Panga, but they had all been removed.

I waited by the shed and tried to prepare myself by pretending that I was an S.A.S. underwater knife fighting hero about to raid the Iranian Embassy. It didn't work, I was still shitting myself. It started to get dark and I could hear the preparations for supper. That bloody great knife didn't seem so big now. It was time to move. Oh, bugger bugger, bugger; I moved.

I crept around the front of the house. The goon was sitting on a chair on the veranda. I waited. Everybody was going in to eat, so the knife went in! I covered his mouth with my right hand and pulled that knife across his neck. Then again, but this time to one side to cut the other artery. He had struggled but Fred was really with it. As soon as the guard started to make the slightest noise, someone had dropped a load of cutlery in the kitchen. attracting everybody's attention. Thankfully it was over. I walked around the body avoiding the blood.

I wiped my hands on his shirt, drew the Browning, cocked the hammer and waited by the French windows. I waited. I waited. Then the scream as one of the women got a tureen of almost boiling soup on her lap. I stepped in. Fred was in the way.

I stepped past him at the same time pushing him to one side. The two other goons and the woman from the island went for their guns. Marie was standing up and was still screaming. I fired three rounds; one at each of them. Then I double tapped each of them in turn. That did it. They were ex members of the organisation. Marie continued to scream but soundlessly. Albert came in and threw a bucket of water over her. He then dragged her into the shower and turned it on. I picked up one of the guns off the floor and gave it to him and told him to watch her.

She had stopped screaming; she realised that she wasn't going to die, at least not then and the cold shower water was stopping the burning. Fred and Alphonse were cheering and Tiffany just looked at me with her mouth agape. Then she smiled. Then she jumped up and jumped on me wrapping her arms and legs around me. I almost fell over. This was not the actions of the refined young woman that her father imagined her to be.

"Sorry about the holes in the table and floor. Alphonse just waved my apology away, and smiled. He along with Fred dragged the bodies over to the one outside and reset the table.

"We've cooked dinner and we're damn well going to have it. Besides we're got something to celebrate." Tiffany phoned daddy and told him that she had been rescued by a hero; that's me by the way.

I didn't sleep much that night, I wasn't allowed to.

CHAPTER 19

A visit to Old Friends & a Visit from Old Friends

I woke up. Woke up? I hadn't been allowed to sleep. I woke up early, more tired than when I went to bed. Everyone except Tiffany was awake. I had a hot shower while I had my chance and sat down and had coffee. Fred had decided that Jean needed the company and was using a wheelbarrow to move the bodies.

I had to think. What were we to do? I turned and looked at Marie. She had spent an uncomfortable night, sitting in a full bath of cold water watched over by each of the guys in turn. I almost felt sorry for her, she had been out of her depth all along. Then I remembered Jimmy, and that she probably had plans for Igor. Any compassion for her just evaporated away. I would have no compunction in using her and then discarding her. She looked at me and read my mind. She said that she would do anything that I wanted, anything.

I told her to shut up and I continued thinking. The first that I knew of Tiffany being awake was when I felt a kiss on my cheek and a comment about me continuing to think, because that was what I was good at, followed by howls of laughter. Then it went quiet again.

I reckoned that there were only about fourteen members of the organisation left in the country to worry about. The two hot-shots and two or three other key figures; the rest would be goons. I still didn't know what they were after, and I'd find out before I got blown around by the winds of fate again.

I told the guys to watch Marie and to put a watch out on the road. I also told them to hide the Toyota, Everything and everybody else had been tidied up. I went to bed. It was going to be a tiring night and I needed my rest. It's not what you think.

I woke up at four o'clock went to fetch the Yamaha. I fuelled up and then cleaned the Browning, albeit a bit late, and the other weapons. I looked at the goon's weapons. Glock 17s and Heckler & Koch M.P.5s; the latest fashion. I took Marie's Mini-Uzi with all three spare mags. I would take the M 79 and leave the P-14. I was ready to rock-and-roll.

I phone the Senior Partner in London. "Nobody's looking for you. I still haven't got your passport, and your name's still mud with the authorities. I now hate this bloody cell phone. Anybody can phone me day or night. What am I, some sort of do-gooder?"

I laughed, "Hang onto it until I return to the U.K.," and rang off.

We had dinner before I left for M'eni's cop shop. I wanted to leave in the dark. I was going to visit White Shirt, I was sure that he would be delighted to see me. Oh, yes, where were those pliers?

I arrived fairly early and crept up the compound, Uzi in the shoulder, pointing down, just as I had been taught, M 79 loaded across my back. I crept up to a new replaced office without tripping over the rubbish tip, this time. The office light was on but the place was otherwise deserted. I looked in.

There was Y'all tied to a chair. Both hands looked a mess. His face looked pretty bad too. Someone had been pretty busy with a set of pliers. Tough, couldn't have happened to a nicer bloke, ha! ha! I saw White Shirt standing with his back to the door saying something to Y'all. I ducked out of the way. He hadn't seen me. I'd been lucky, and I wanted to stay lucky.

I picked up one of the many booze bottles on the tip, and crept around to the front of the hut. I walked in and said hello, and as he turned, I hit him as hard as I could across the side of the head. He collapsed. For good measure, and because I was feeling vindictive, I kicked him in the family jewels, hard. He didn't feel a thing; you can't have everything, but maybe he'd feel it when he woke up.

Y'all didn't seem that surprised to see me. "Welcome. I've been expecting y'all. Y'all arrived just on time. May ah help y'all to tie mah colleague here to a chair?" I wasn't yet willing to untie him.

He realised that I could kill them both and no-one would be any the wiser for it. He could also see that I had changed, so he started talking without me asking. He told me, "Ah'll start at the beginning." That's always a good place to start.

"Y'all were set up by an organisation that has recently gone into crime. It was this organisation which initially trained me, in Texas. They're pretending to support both the rebel movement, especially one run by a man called Kabila, and Mobuto's Government. Mah colleague here works for them. Y'all were used to provide the Government with a rebel training expert while the real one made his way to the rebels. Y'all were moved across the border, and the vehicle in which y'all were travelling was supposed to have been ambushed by those four idiots." So far, so good. "A schism developed in the organisation and a group broke away, most of whom were killed. Ah don't know why." I did, money! But, I didn't tell him. He continued. "Ah found out about the expert and had y'all picked up at the border. Your kidnappers had been shot in the process."

"Y'all were to be taken, first by Presidential car to Kisangani, then by plane to Kinshasa, when y'all were again ambushed but by those four French idiots, this time. The gendarmes had found y'all, so mah colleague was unable to dispose of y'all, and had to send y'all to me. That explained how I had got to M'eni."

He went on, "Initially, ah thought that y'all were a really well trained operative, then ah realised that y'all were an innocent. Ah wanted to confuse the organisation into believing that the security forces believed that y'all were the expert. Y'all were about to be allowed to escape when y'all escaped for real. Ah had given orders that y'all should escape, but mah two operatives were actually in the pay of mah colleague, and wanted y'all dead. Ah ignored y'all being a serpent in the bush, if y'all remember? I remembered. "Y'all did me a great service by killing them."

"Y'all were on the loose causing confusion, allowing me to investigate without suspicion. He made no mention of Tiffany, and I thought that he hadn't made the connection.

"Ah guessed that y'all had shot up the police post." I said something about admiring the new office. He nodded and continued. "This organisation is planning to take over the country. It plans to destroy Mobuto's credibility with something, maybe a photograph. They're going to encourage Kabila's rebels to rise up against the government, and then destroy whichever side is the victor."

"They'll then install a puppet president and rip off the country just like Mobuto. They're now in the final stages of this plan, but we have both helped to screw them."

He continued on a personal note. "You'll have to understand that ah think that Mobuto is evil and that ah have done some horrific things in his name. The problem is that Zaire doesn't have a Museveni and so any leader of Zaire is going to be a typical African tyrant. The people who always get hurt are the poor and the only protection for them is to stop any civil strife. They'll remain poor but at least they won't get killed just for being in the way. Ah hope that one day, we'll have a Museveni, but ah doubt that it will be in mah lifetime."

"We'll have to destroy the remaining elements, so would y'all mind cutting me loose?" I did just that. "Thank y'all. Mah colleague has sent the gendarmes on a wild goose chase but that they will be back shortly. Y'all have obviously entered the country unofficially, and y'all had better get out unofficially, so y'all had better go before they get back. Could ah do y'all a favour in thanks?"

I thought about all those bearer bonds in Tiffany's safe deposit, and how some were going to get lost. Diamonds would be difficult to dispose of. "No, there? nothing you can do." Then I thought a bit. "Yes, there is, you can do two things. Firstly, Alphonse and Albert don't really know what is going on. They are harmless."

"Ah know all about that, their man Fred, is one of mah informers. The other?"

"The second is to give a second hand London bus a trial. I think that the Foreign Office thought that I had screwed up the deal and so they are causing me real problems. I think that a Zairean bus driver will tip over one of those double-deckers on the first day; but that will solve my problems with the Foreign Office."

He laughed, "Ah'll see what ah can do, but in return, y'all must leave Marie at the house. Ah've always fancied a French mistress."

We said goodbye. "Good luck and take care of your young lady." I left.

I've got back to the house at about one o'clock. They were worried. The hot-shots had phoned a satellite phone which the goons had brought with them. Marie had tried her best, maybe? Tiffany was sure that they had smelled a rat. Fred had also found a briefcase under the mattress. He thought it may be important. It was.

It contained a photo of Mobuto having sex with a dog. It was so obviously a forgery, it was laughable. There was also a big soft bag containing diamonds. I split it, giving everyone a share. My share was biggest because I was the hero. Nobody argued. I took Fred to one side when I gave him his share, and told him about Y'all's request relating to Marie, and for Fred to hand her to him. I also gave him the photo to give to Y'all.

He told me, "My commander has some very interesting sexual practices, and I can think of no-one more deserving than Marie." I issued all the weapons keeping Marie's Uzi, and told the others to get up to the cottage and be prepared to use the mines.

"You've to get out as soon as you hear firing and get straight to the border. Tiffany, you have your passport, so there won't be any problem. You all have enough diamonds to start a new life if necessary. I gave Tiffany my diamonds and most of the dollars that I had kept from Folkestone to look after.

I took her to one side. "There's numbered bank accounts and bearer bonds in your joint deposit box. It's currently under litigation. Give the list of accounts to Uncle Sam but keep ten percent, even fifteen per cent of the bonds as a finder's fee." She knew that this was my endowment to her if I didn't make it. She turned away and started crying.

I left and got on the bike without looking back. I rode to my look-out spot near the marshy area. I left the Uzi on the bike and had the P-14 and M 79 ready and waiting. I waited.

It was a beautiful sunrise, and I thought that it was too beautiful to die, but I stayed and waited. I soon heard the whine of a single Casspir and that of the gearbox of a Land Rover. They were coming. I waited nervously.

I had managed to survive a series of incidents. I felt that planning and luck had been on my side. This was going to be my first true battle. I had not joined the T.A. for this battle, but it had long ago trained me for it. I thought about Tiffany, and that relaxed me somewhat until I heard the goons, fast approaching.

The Casspir was leading the Land Rover. I waited until the Casspir was opposite the middle mine and pushed the plunger. All three went off simultaneously. Both vehicles rolled. I had blasted the Land Rover badly, but I had only destroyed a wheel of the Casspir and pushed it over with the blast. It had performed exactly as designed; the goons in the back scrambled out wearing those blasted Rambo T-shirts. They started to spread out. They were about at the range limit of the M 79. I gave them one before they spread out too much and reloaded. Half of them soon lost interest in the proceedings. The other half kept on coming. One person from the Land Rover joined them.

I recognised one of the hot-shots, the Australian. I acquired him in the scope of the P-14. Gotcha! He went down. I started to receive fire. I moved. Someone was firing a belt fed machine gun at my previous position. Another grenade soon stopped that. I moved again.

It would be a waste to use another grenade at single targets so I reverted to the P-14. I hit another two and reloaded, before I ran back to the Bike. I rode back to the house and waited.

They were advancing carefully. I heard the Toyota start up. Good, they were getting away now. I waited. I sniped another one. I heard the Land Rover start. Maybe I hadn't damaged it as badly as I thought. With the two advancing on me, I now had a further one to four goons to deal with. If I stayed in the house I would have been trapped. I left.

I drove the bike towards the cottage and waited. I could now see what I was up against. There were six of them. A driver and a machine gunner in the Rover. Ahead and to either side were two pairs of goons. I looked again, no more.

I drove up to the cottage and waited. The M 79 was loaded and sighted for the expected range. I waited. Just as one pair was along side the mines, I pushed the plunger. I shot a grenade at the Rover, but missed. However the effect did not miss the machine gunner. I looked at the effect of the mines, I must have at least wounded the other pair but I could hear and see nothing. I took the M 79 and P-14 to the bike and took up the Uzi. I found some cover and waited.

The pair were advancing, giving each other covering fire. They were skirmishing up to the cottage. I waited until they were opposite me, and then double tapped them both. I used semi auto fire, they used fully auto. I know that the rear one never stood a chance. The front one had to turn around to face me but she started to fire too early and her H&K M.P.5 was set on fully auto. She was too busy trying to control it, and was firing high. I didn't. Both of my bullets went just where they were supposed to. She went down. Although I had only fired four rounds, I changed mags and waited.

I knew that there was one more person, the driver. I could hear slight moaning. I carefully went down towards the sound. It was the Canadian. As I thought, he wasn't wounded at all! He was hoping that I would fall for it. I didn't. I could see that he had taken good cover. I also saw that I could rush him from the flank. I had cover for everything up to the last four or five meters. It took me about half a hour to reach my start line. I set the Uzi on full auto. I started to sprint. I aimed low and fired a burst, the barrel rose; I aimed low again and fired another burst. I was on top of him. I was at his feet. I aimed at his feet and fired another but longer burst. I hit him five times from his feet to his head.

I had fired a total of twelve rounds so I changed mags again. I waited. Nothing. I still waited. Still nothing. I could hear the faint sound of sirens. The gendarmes must be coming. Time to go. I got up to go to the bike only to find that I was looking down the barrel of a twelve bore pump action.

The Australian was holding it. The first person who I had drilled with the P-14. He thumbed his chest and I could see that he was wearing a very large bullet resistant vest with some sort of hard material down the front. He was looking very red faced and now I really recognised him. He was the fellow with whom I had a confrontation over a taxi to visit the gorillas. "Drop your weapons."

I thought about Tiffany; I wasn't going to go down without a fight. I threw down the Uzi. It didn't work. It didn't go off. He knew what I had tried to do and laughed. "You carry a Browning. Luckily I had been about to reach for the S&W. "Throw it over here. I carefully drew it, passed it to my other hand and tossed the Browning at his feet. He was starting to speak, but he was distracted by the Browning landing at his feet. I had turned away from him, as in fear, just before I threw the Browning. As it landed, I drew the snubby and fired two shots under my arm and through my jacket. I fired low and hit him once in the thigh. I pulled the snubby clear and fired another shot and it went into his open mouth. I didn't need any others.

His dead eyes looked up at me in horror, as though he realised that he had picked the wrong man.

I picked up the Browning and the Uzi, reloaded the S&W and hid the shotgun in the shed. I got on the bike and left.

CHAPTER 20

The Border & Rewards

I caught up with them about halfway to the concession. They stopped when they saw my dust and waited. They had done this every time they saw a motor bike in the mirror, at Tiffany's insistence. This was the forth time. When they saw that it was me, there was a cheer and Tiffany started to jump up and down.

Anyway, after the festivities, I phoned her father. I told him the situation. "Your contacts may wish to send some hard men to the mine, lots of them and very hard, under some pretext or another to apprehend the bad guys. I don't think that the authorities will make a big song and dance if the bad guys all have fatal accidents in the process Anyway, it's no longer my problem.

"I'll pass it on." and then asked, "When am I going to see you?

"We've got to get out of the country first and then I am going to put Tiffany on a plane to the States. I got to go to the U.K. first and see if I can't get to the States in my own name. It is always better to be legitimate, if one can. As a lawyer, you can only agree." He spoke to Tiffany and then rung off.

I then phoned the other lawyer, the Senior Partner. "I'm bloody glad to hear that your safe, and you've got Tiffany with you? Well done!"

"Tell your chum that I may have arranged for Zaire to test a double-decker. Tell him that the official that I spoke to, agreed that the bloody thing'll fall on its side on the first day of testing. They had better be prepared for that." He rung off mumbling something about bloody cell phones.

To cut a long story short, we got over the border and made it safely to Kampala. I got Tiffany on the next flight to the States while I went back to London via Amsterdam where I sold the diamonds.

In London I phoned the Senior Partner on his cell phone, for the last time. "I have your passport. I can never repay you, especially, after what you've done for Tiffany. I'll courier the passport immediately to your solicitor. Just part of the do-gooder service. Now I can now jump on this bloody phone!"

I realised that there was nothing to keep me in the U.K.. I phoned the York consultancy to decline their kind offer just before I boarded my flight.

I phoned Tiffany from the airport, I'm taking the bus."

She told me, "Nice people don't take the bus."

"I'm not nice people."

She agreed, "I know, but take the train anyway. I'll meet you at the station."

I stayed at her father's place. Strange, he left his bedroom door open all night. I wonder why?

The next morning I visited the geeks. They were really glad to see me. "Word's got around and we've now got more work than we can handle. The shareholder/directors asked, "Would you like to join us as a director with a ten percent shareholding?" They needed my brain or something.

"If you agree, you'll run a new office in New Orleans. We're also going to open offices in Seattle and Chicago. They didn't think that I would like to stay in the other three offices. "You can even do environmental work to from time to time, if you like." They had hacked into the Manchester international consultant's data base and read my C.V..

How could I refuse? "But there's going be a problem about a Green Card."

"Problem, what problem?" They showed me one with my name on it. "Contacts." they said, "Legal contacts."

About the Author

Hamish Clarke was born in Dundee, but his parents moved to Nottingham when he was 4. He has been an insurance clerk since he was 18 years old, but as a result of his work, he has had the opportunity to meet a number of really interesting people who have been involved in unusual activities in sub-equatorial Africa, and elsewhere.

The stories told by these people have resulted in this story.

This is neither a Biography, nor is it based on real events.

Lightning Source UK Ltd.
Milton Keynes UK
UKOW05f0759020115

243798UK00001B/9/P